Read Between the Lines

a novel by

Jill Breugem

READ BETWEEN THE LINES

© Copyright 2016 Jill Breugem

Edited by Darla Wright

Cover Design by Adriana Breugem

Heart Doodle: Shuttershock/Vectortion #454507

Formatted by Wendi Temporado

All rights reserved. This book or any portion thereof may not be reproduced or used in any manner whatsoever without the express written permission of the publisher.

This is a work of fiction. Names, characters, businesses, places, events and incidents are either the products of the author's imagination or used in a fictitious manner. Any resemblance to actual persons, living or dead, or actual events is purely coincidental.

Table of Contents

Chapter 1 1

Chapter 2 13

Chapter 3 25

Chapter 4 31

Chapter 5 41

Chapter 6 49

Chapter 7 57

Chapter 8 63

Chapter 9 73

Chapter 10 79

Chapter 11 89

Chapter 12 97

Chapter 13 103

Chapter 14 109

Chapter 15 119

Chapter 16 127

Chapter 17 133

Chapter 18 141

Chapter 19 149

Chapter 20 155

Chapter 21 161

Chapter 22 167

Chapter 23 177

Chapter 24 181

Chapter 25 187

Chapter 26 193

Chapter 27 201

Chapter 28 209

Chapter 29 217

Chapter 30 225

Acknowledgements

With a grateful heart, I thank ALL of my friends and family for your support! From the leaders and motivators, to the fellow dream chasers, I thank you for your encouragement through this exciting chapter of my life. xo

Some special mentions:

Darla W.- Thank you for all of your help, dedication, and support. I am so fortunate that my boy brought us together years ago. Your friendship means the world!

Doug D. - It all began from a conversation we had one day. You challenged me to think about the big picture and do something solely for me. Thank you for the nudge!

Alana C. - My faithful reader of tiny excerpts and texts over the last year and half. Your cheering and guidance made me smile along the way!

Jessica B. and Stephen W. - Thank you for your endless insight and advice!

Katie I. - You always think positive and believe in the best for me! From day one of this process you were cheering me on. #soulsister

Moira W. - Some time spent with you - and all is well in my world again. Thanks for your amazing feedback and expert advice along the way!

Tina S. Friend/Therapist/Comedian/Doctor/Teacher/Overall Rock Star - oh the hats you wear for me my friend... "Rise up this mornin',smiled with the risin' sun,three little birds, pitch by my doorstep, singin' sweet songs, of melodies pure and true, sayin, this is my message to you" ~ Bob Marley

Mom and Dad - Your love and support mean more than you will ever know. I hope I make you half as proud, as I am to call you my parents. Happy 50 years! Love you!

I dedicate this book to the loves of my life: Jaap, Adriana, Alex, and our furbaby, Lucy.

Jaap - Your love, support, and belief in my abilities (with everything I do) is unwavering. "You and me together, we could do anything, Baby"~ Dave Matthews Band.

Adriana - My cover designer! Your amazing creativity is matched by your intellect, beauty, and your compassion for all. You are one amazing package of a human being and I am so proud of you.

Alex - You inspire me every day to do better. One day you will understand that we are all better people for knowing YOU my sweet boy.

Lucy - My lovely girl and dedicated companion for the last ten years. You are never far, especially when I need you most.

Chapter 1

Revelations

Sadie tucked the golden strand of hair behind her ear and stretched her arms above her head. She stared blankly at the screen. She had been up for several hours but completely out of routine lately and hadn't gone for her usual run. She had no motivation was a little hung-over and couldn't concentrate enough to type one sentence. She had gone out with her best friend Ally to the movies and they ended up drinking red wine back at her apartment and gabbing until the wee hours. That is when Sadie confessed to Ally that she was in love with someone, and had been for some time.

"I can't believe you waited this long to tell me!" Ally had said and admitted that she knew something was up.

"Well, I think I always have felt something. And recently, something just clicked in me, I didn't want to just be his friend anymore." she smiled.

"Well, I am absolutely sure, if the circumstances were different for both of you over the years, you would have had this revelation a long time ago." Ally topped up their glasses with a vintage Australian Shiraz. "You've both had the worst timing for being single when the other wasn't." Ally picked up her phone and put on a Van Morrison playlist over the Bluetooth speakers.

"You noticed that?" Sadie picked up her wine and held it close to her chest, breathing in the the red berry scent. She started to hum along to "Sweet Thing".

"Oh ya, for years we all have had bets on when you two would get together," Ally confessed with a shrug and a laugh.

"What? Who?"

Ally tilted her head back and laughed. "Oh just a few people. Samantha, Piper, Mason…" Sadie rolled her eyes and interrupted, knowing Ally

READ BETWEEN THE LINES

wasn't done. "What about our working relationship?" Sadie asked.

"That ship sailed when you two became such close friends years ago. I honestly have no idea how you two haven't gotten together before now," Ally said matter of fact.

As her mind continued to wander over last night's conversation, she considered that maybe Ally was right. Levi and Sadie always had a good time when they were together. Heck they were always together. Levi had been there through the success of her books, through the sadness that followed each break up, and through some personal tragedies. He really was one of her best friends.

The cursor blinked in the same position as it had been for the last thirty minutes. Maybe this wasn't going to happen today? She was always writing, but at the moment, she had a serious case of writer's block. Her creative mind usually had a myriad of storylines going at once, but lately nothing was inspiring her. Nothing was speaking to her so loudly that she had to get it on paper, or had to wake up in the night and scribble it down for fear of forgetting in the morning, which she had done with all of her books.

Sadie Fisher had written a half a dozen romance novels, making the New York Times

Bestseller list each time. Lately, she had not so much as written a single sentence and people were getting concerned, including Levi Townsend, who was also her literary agent. She had promised him that she would have something for the editor by September. That was under four months away, and she had nothing, not even an idea.

She picked up the glass ball that was holding some papers down on her desk. Swirling it around in her palm, she wished it was a crystal ball, helping her to see the future. It was a gift from her cousin who had brought it back from the Netherlands because she knew how much Sadie would love the shades of turquoise and blue blown throughout. The colours were found in her apartment, mixed in with shades of charcoal and light grey. She set the glass ball back down on the papers, ran her fingers through her golden hair, and piled it on the top of her head in a messy bun.

Her office was a bright space with a large window facing the downtown core. It inspired her to look out at the city and write. Sheer white curtains hung on either side. Her sleek white furniture was anchored by a plush turquoise shag rug. A large, silver, vintage sunburst mirror hung on one wall and built-in bookshelves lined the other. She loved this space and had written some of her best work in this room.

Her wrist vibrated with a message on her smartwatch. Without even looking Sadie undid the clasp and dropped the watch to the cushy floor below. She winced slightly as she heard it bounce on the rug. It had been a gift from Levi for her birthday back in April. It was supposed to make it even easier for him to get in touch with her, as well as keep her organized. Pressure; pressure is what it made her feel.

Levi was the best agent in the city. Everyone wanted to work with him. He became a literary agent after working at a publishing company for several years and having contact with many successful writers. She remembered their first meeting. She had been in awe of him. He was confident, charming and gorgeous. He had a mop of wavy, blonde hair, skin kissed by the summer sun, clear blue eyes lined with thick lashes, a chiseled jaw, and a big beautiful smile. It was his personality that took it all over the top. He was thoughtful and so funny; he had a way of making her feel so many things all at the same time.

They had a special relationship, and it confused many. When they were out she would get called his wife or girlfriend and would quickly correct them while Levi would sit back calmly with a crooked grin and a wink, not bothered in the least. Levi was in a relationship right now, and when he had been single, Sadie wasn't. If there was ever a thought of crossing the professional line, bad timing had followed them both. There was also the issue of not knowing if each other felt the same. Yes they had chemistry and flirted, but what if that is all that it was?

Sadie stood up, stretched, and bent her body forward to touch her toes. She thought about going to yoga. It always made her feel better. Maybe she would throw on a video now and do some since she had no focus. Or meditate. Maybe she would meditate. Thoughts whirled around in her mind and her watch and her phone vibrated.

There was a knock at the door. Ugh, this distraction was not helping. Grabbing her sweater she threw it over her tank top and ran her fingers under her eyes. "Coming!" She called as there was another knock at the door. Her stomach landed in her throat when she looked through the peephole and saw it was Levi. He had a key but always knocked first. Sadie had given him a key years ago to make it easier coming into the building so she didn't have to buzz him up every time. He came

READ BETWEEN THE LINES

over at least every other day. That's how close they were.

"Good morning Levi ..." her voice trailed off as he walked past her with tea and coffee and what looked like breakfast. Mmmm, he smelled good. A subtle mix of sandalwood and orange, and she never tired of it.

"Sadie, it's a dungeon in here! Open the drapes or turn some lights on," Levi said as he went to the kitchen with our breakfast.

"It's not dark in the office. I've been busy. Thanks for the tea, I needed that," Sadie said.

"You better have been busy. They're hounding me for a sneak peek at your new book, and we only have a few months before I," he said, pausing for effect, "no, you, promised the editor." Levi didn't miss a beat as he continued, "and I know you have the next best story coming!" Levi kissed her cheek as he walked past Sadie to the office. She followed behind him. He was wearing a pair of jeans with a navy blue shirt that made his blue eyes even more intense.

"Well, it's coming..." She lied.

"So, can I see what you have so far?" he asked as he walked towards the laptop sitting on her desk.

7

"No!" Sadie leapt in front of him, blocking him from the desk. Their bodies collided and reactively he wrapped one arm around her waist and one hand on the desk, to steady them. Sadie closed the laptop quickly. "You know how I feel about that, it's not ready." She could feel his breath on her earlobe and the smoothness of clean shaven cheek as she turned to speak over her shoulder.

Levi pretended to reach for the lid of the laptop and laughed as he teased her. He let go of her waist and backed up a couple steps. Her body felt the instant loss of his warmth and she turned around to face him. Trying to look stern with one eyebrow raised, she shook her finger no. In turn he gave her an adorable grin. Perfect teeth. Perfect mouth. Perfect jaw. Oh man she was in trouble.

"Okay, okay, I know how you are. It must be something," Levi said with his arms raised in defeat. "I thought maybe you were in a slump. You haven't shared anything with me yet, and you usually do," his voice trailed off.

Levi almost stepped on the watch lying on the floor, picked it up, looked at her, and asked, "Now, how is this going to notify you on the floor, Sadie?"

"It must have slipped off," Sadie said and snatched the smartwatch from him, putting it back on her wrist. "What are you doing for lunch today? We could go grab some Thai?" she asked, hopeful.

"I'm meeting Barbara and some of her friends in the distillery district at 1:00. They're in town from Chicago. Hey, you should come," Levi said.

"Oh no, that's ok, I'm busy, I have lots to do," Sadie mumbled as she turned her back to him and went back to her desk. The last person she felt like being around was his snobby girlfriend who took every opportunity to rub it in her face that Levi was hers. Sadie continued to be polite and respectful for his sake, but what she really wanted to do was deck Barbara. Barbara…even thinking her name made her growl.

"Why are you growling?" Levi laughed, she hadn't realized she did it out loud. "Come on, you should take a break," he said as he stepped behind her and put his hands on her shoulders and ran them down her arms in a comforting way. "Come have the croissant I brought for you." She shivered, and he noticed. What was wrong with her? Sadie shrugged away from him and quickly sat down in her chair.

"Sadie, are you okay? I can tell Barb that I can't make it."

"No, no it's fine, I'm just tired. I was out late with Ally." Professing my love for you, she thought. "Drank a little too much wine."

Levi came around the desk, grabbed a chair and sat down beside her. "Sadie, look at me," he said with concern.

Sadie lifted her eyes slowly and met his. They held for a few moments. He was so close she could almost taste the mint gum he was chewing. His expression changed from his usual friendly agent concern to something she had never noticed before. His eyes were almost closing as he looked at her mouth. He licked his lips and let out a long sigh. For a moment she thought of telling him. But like so many times before, fear stepped in.

Levi broke their gaze and looked down at the floor, pushed his chair back and took a deep breath. Clearly this close contact had made him uncomfortable.

"You aren't letting the stress of the book getting to you, are you?" he asked. He was so far thought Sadie.

"Well, I have just been pouring myself into this book, probably not eating or sleeping the best. I am just going to write for a bit and then go out for a run this afternoon, maybe yoga later." Sadie rattled, trying to ease the tension in the room.

Levi looked at her; he opened his mouth to say something but stopped.

"I better get going then. Tomorrow morning we have a meeting with Piper to review the dates. I'll swing by and pick you up at 8:30, ok?"

"Sounds great. Thanks again for breakfast." He looked at her softly, gave her a quick hug, walked to the door, and let himself out.

Sadie locked the apartment door behind him and leaned up against it. She thought about the meeting in the morning and started to cry. Was it exhaustion? Was she that hungover she had brought herself to tears? Time of the month? Or was it that she had to tell him and the editor that she had nothing written, not even an outline. She was screwed. She should have tried to push the meeting out a couple weeks, but she had already done it once and knew that wouldn't sit well with either of them.

She got a text message from Levi (already). "Don't forget to eat…I know how you get when you are absorbed in writing a new book."

"I won't"

"If you lose so much as a pound, I will have pizza delivered daily!"

"Lol, oh geez...alright alright....you're so bossy"

"I mean it Sade, not a pound."

"You.Are.Ridiculous. Ttyl"

An idea came to her just then, and she walked over and opened her laptop.

Chapter 2

The Meeting

Her hand reached out blindly to her bedside table to grab her phone to turn off the alarm. She didn't know why she had selected a king size bed; she had to roll several times towards the table because she had a habit of sleeping right in the middle. She rubbed her eyes and stretched, pushing the layers of soft blankets away. She had to get in the shower before Levi got here.

She had stayed up late last night and made progress with her book. After Levi left, the story just flowed out of her. She was nowhere near ready to pass it on to her editor, but she had made great headway. Something about the way she felt when he left yesterday sent her into a spin, which then sent her straight to her computer to let it all out. She didn't know if the story would ever see the light of day, but the fact she was at least writing, meant something.

Sadie wrapped a towel around her head and another around her body. She went into her walk in closet to figure out what she was going to wear for the meeting with Piper. She settled on a simple black and white striped maxi dress. She laid it across the centre island in her walk-in closet and opened her lingerie drawer.

When she made her money and designed her penthouse apartment in the very trendy building just north of the downtown core, her closet was very important in the design. This closet had your typical hanging area, shelves for handbags, mini closets for jewellery, hooks for scarves, full length mirrors, and the beautiful centre island filled with drawers on every side. This room was bigger than some bedrooms and was a very extravagant request.

There was a knock at the door.

"Shoot!" She wasn't even dressed yet. It was too early for Levi, who could it be? She peaked through the hole to see him on the other side. What was he doing here already? She was only wearing a towel, dripping wet, and Levi was almost an hour early.

Opening the door only a crack, Sadie said, "What are doing here already, it's only 7:45."

Pushing the door open with a grin, he said, "Yes I know, I'm taking you for breakfast." Levi watched her as she squealed and ran to her room wearing only a towel. "You should get some clothes on," he teased and winked at her on her way past.

"Very funny, you're early!" she called from the bedroom.

He smiled to himself. She was right, but truth be told he couldn't wait to see her. She was probably his best friend; in fact she was the first person he thought of when he woke up in the morning and the last at night when he closed his eyes. A corny thing to think, and not the smartest for someone who was her agent and dating someone else. He knew a piece of his heart would always belong to Sadie, regardless of who he was dating at the time. Which was not fair to the women he dated.

He remembered the first time he met her because she had completely mesmerized him. She had published her first novel and it went straight to number one on the New York Times Best Sellers list. His friend Oliver had introduced them thinking she could use an agent with the type of success and attention she was getting. They met for a drink and although Oliver warned him she was beautiful, he had no idea her beauty would be matched by her intelligence and fantastic sense of humour. They must have laughed the entire evening.

"I won't be long," she said as she peeked out of her bedroom, dressed, but still with a towel on her head. "Are we meeting Piper at the office on Richmond? … Or?"

"Yes, I told her we would go to her office. Where do you feel like eating this morning?" Levi asked.

"I know it's going the opposite direction, but I would love a smoothie from the juice bar over on Church."

"Sure," Levi responded.

Levi walked to the window and looked over Yonge St as he heard the hair dryer start up; morning rush hour was in full swing and there was a lot of activity below. They had an hour before their meeting; a smoothie was probably the best choice. When he left yesterday he knew he wanted to see her before the meeting so he could go into it prepared. Usually he has more of an idea of where his authors are at, but Sadie had been keeping him

READ BETWEEN THE LINES

in the dark this time. He didn't know what was up, but he was going to get to the bottom of it. This was an important deadline, Sadie hadn't put out anything in over a year, and the publishing house said this book would determine if they would continue her contract. Sure he would lose commission, but he didn't care about that with Sadie. It made no difference to his career if Sadie ever wrote again. He wouldn't want her to stop writing because writing was Sadie. Writing was in the fabric of her being, woven through her heart and soul. She simply HAD TO WRITE.

Sadie had written in journals since she was a child, and one night last winter they had lain on her bedroom floor going through diary after diary. They drank a couple bottles of wine as they giggled and cried (her more than him) through the many years of her life on paper. He had never felt closer to anyone in his life. If she hadn't been fresh out of her relationship with Ethan, and he just started a relationship with Barbara, he may have made a move that night. The wine, the music, the mood, everything was perfect, and reading the personal details of her life had made him just love her more.

"I'm ready," Sadie said from behind him. It didn't matter if he saw her every day, each time he did it was like the first. She was breathtaking. Her

17

JILL BREUGEM

long golden hair hung in soft layers around her shoulders and her blue eyes had this infectious sparkle. Her skin was still showing some of the tan she got from a spring trip she went on with her friend Ally to Bahamas.

"What's wrong?" she said as she looked down at her dress.

"Not a single thing," he said as he lifted his gaze to meet hers. He grabbed her by the hand and they exited her apartment.

Once in his car she turned to him and asked, "So how was your visit with Babs and friends?"

Levi could hear the animosity in her tone. He knew that Sadie and Barbara didn't really see eye to eye. He wasn't sure why they got off on such a bad foot, but they had never gotten over it. Barbara was a little high maintenance but they got along pretty well. He wasn't sure where the relationship was going just yet. He answered, "It was good, didn't make it a long visit."

He headed south on Yonge and turned left onto Bloor Street. Traffic was heavy, but normal for this time of day.

"Wearing your watch again I see?" he changed the subject.

READ BETWEEN THE LINES

"Ya, it was a gift from this guy…and he might get pissy if I don't wear it…"

"It's a great watch!"

"Yes, I know, I do love it…"

"The usual?"

"Yes please" she answered as he pulled up in front of the juice bar. She got comfortable and turned on the radio. She changed his station from current pop hits to a country station. She had grown up in rural Ontario and although she loved all kinds of music, country music was in her blood. She was convinced if she hadn't been a writer she would have done something in the music industry.

Sadie was starting to get butterflies about the meeting with Piper in twenty minutes. She knew Piper would want to know information about the book, specifically the storyline and the characters. Sadie was usually ready for this, but this time it was personal. It would take more than a few drinks before she would spill on the details. What was she thinking making a love story loosely based on her relationship with Levi? Levi (and Piper for that matter) would surely guess regardless of the changed names.

"So did Piper give you an agenda for the meeting this morning? What she is looking for?"

Sadie asked as Levi climbed back into the car and passed her smoothie.

"Sadie," he said and looked at her before pulling into traffic. "You have been to a ton of these meetings. Seriously?"

"Oh, I know, I'm just nervous," Sadie explained.

"Well, nothing much has changed. She'll want to work out some dates, deadlines, promotional," Levi continued "as well as brief synopsis of the storyline."

Sadie looked out her window, feeling the heat build in her cheeks. Nausea set in as she realized she was in trouble and had to think fast. She had no choice but to either make something up quick or tell them the actual plot and hope it went over their heads. What if it didn't? Wasn't she expecting to let Levi read it eventually? Isn't that why she wrote it? Let the book do the talking, say everything she needed to say and couldn't?

Think fast, she thought to herself as he put the car in park. They had ten minutes to spare and Levi pulled out his phone to check messages. She pretended to do the same, as she quickly made up a story about Evan and Mary. Mary a model falls for the experienced photographer. They fall in love instantly, but Mary's family doesn't think he is good enough after a highly-publicized incident with an actress, and so he must prove himself. That's it!

"Ready?" Levi asked as he opened his door and ran around to hers. He was always the gentleman, and it never failed to impress her. She couldn't help thinking that someone like Barbara didn't deserve him.

They walked into the beautiful modern glass building and reception ushers them right in.

"Sadie!" Piper exclaimed and ran to hug her. "Great to see you girl!"

"You too!" Sadie answered and smiled. Piper had a beautiful crown of corkscrew black curls, with caramel ombre highlights. She was beautiful and had an equally captivating personality. Sadie adored her. Piper was wearing a red and orange bohemian style jumpsuit with thin straps. The outfit is daring, but Piper pulls it off effortlessly and it looks amazing against her creamy skin. Piper is only wearing lip gloss, but with her amber coloured eyes, high cheekbones and full lips, she doesn't need anything else. Piper is gorgeous, and Sadie always thought she should be a model.

The next hour flew by as Sadie tells them the story she literally just made up. Thankfully they

JILL BREUGEM

buy it. They settle on some promotional dates and arrange to meet again in a month.

"Don't forget the barbecue!" said Piper.

"Looking forward to it, Piper!"

Once back in the car, Levi says, "Book sounds great Sadie, can't wait to read it." He looks at her quietly for a few moments. "Why does it seem like you're hiding something?"

"What are you talking about? I'm not hiding anything." Sadie wore her heart on her sleeve when it came to Levi, he always knew. She looked out the window hoping he would just take her word for it.

"Sadie, look at me."

"No." She laughed. Feeling her face flush, it always gave her away.

"Sadie Anne Fisher."

"Nothing, stop it!" She giggled.

"You won't even look at me, and your face is turning red."

"It's because you're asking me to look at you... stop!" She laughed. Sadie was saved by the ringing of Levi's phone over the Bluetooth stereo. The screen showed it was Barbara.

"Hey Barbara."

READ BETWEEN THE LINES

"Hi babe, just calling to say hi, and see how your day is going." Sadie couldn't help but note the time was only 10:00am.

"I'm driving Sadie back up to her apartment. We just got out of a meeting with the publisher."

"Hi Barbara," Sadie said not wanting to be rude.

"Hi Sadie," her tone annoyed.

"I'll call you when I drop Sadie off, okay?"

"Yep," she said curtly and hung up.

"How did you two meet again?" Sadie asked him, with animosity in her tone.

"I was playing golf up at Angus Glen, she was there with a friend."

"And the rest is beautiful history." Sadie nudged him in the side. He smirked, shrugged his shoulders, and let out a chuckle.

"I met her just before you and Ethan broke up." He said it matter of fact, like saying this had any impact on how the story goes.

"Yes, yes you did." He pulled up in front of her building.

"I'll just drop you off at the door okay? I have a meeting at 11:00 out near the airport."

23

JILL BREUGEM

"Of course, thanks for the ride and the breakfast, talk to you later." Sadie hopped out and went to work on her eighth novel. After all, number seven may never get read.

Chapter 3

Writing

Sadie stared out at the city, sipping on her chai tea latte and listening to Ray Lamontagne. She was thinking about how fortunate she had been over the last several years with her books. Her fans had stuck by her side since the first one, and although it would always be special, she was sure this book was going to be her favourite. Some of her best memories were shared within. People might even call it a biography one day.

The haunting sounds of 'Hannah' moved around the apartment like a slow, painful, last dance. She sang along with tears welling up in her eyes, knowing firsthand the ache of wanting someone so badly it hurt. She acknowledged that writing this novel was both therapeutic and punishing to her at the same time; it just made her love, want, and need him even more.

She set down her mug and tapped out a memory. Years ago, just after they started working together, Sadie, Levi, and a pile of their mutual friends ended up in a small nightclub. It was dark, with only a light over the bar and a haze around the dancefloor. The music was amazing, the drinks were flowing, and you couldn't drag Sadie and Levi off of the dancefloor. One familiar song after another they sang along, singing to each other with no inhibition. They moved to the beat, taking breaks only to have a quick drink. During a familiar sixties soul song, he took both of her hands in his, pulling her in close to him. Their cheeks brushed against each other and she can still remember the feeling of his face and the current that went through her.

Her new boyfriend Lenny came over and cut in. Lenny must've seen what was happening because that night on the dance floor they literally forgot everyone else existed. In fact she forgot that Lenny was even there. Sadie and Levi were caught up in the drinks, the music, in each other. The alcohol gave them the courage to dance, while the

READ BETWEEN THE LINES

music gave them the words that they had wanted to say.

Stepping back, Levi reluctantly said "Of course," and let her go. Looking back at Levi watching her as Lenny danced her farther away from him caused an ache in her heart that she had never felt before. They held onto each other's gaze until they were out of each other's view.

At the time, Levi and Sadie's working relationship was still quite new and the fleeting but pivotal moment on the dancefloor was soon forgotten, or at least not talked about. Neither one would broach the subject of that evening, even after Sadie broke up with Lenny. Sadie busied herself writing, book after book, traveling and promoting, and their relationship grew into a respectful and very close platonic friendship.

The more friends and family would tease them, the more they dug in and proved they were just friends. As long as one of them said it, they both believed it. The strength it took over the last seven years was worthy of a medal. Yet here Sadie was seven years after that dance, thinking about the feel of his face against hers like it was yesterday, wondering what if things had been different. What would their lives look like now? Would she have been able to write bestseller after bestseller without the wanting in her heart?

Her phone chimed with a message. Looking down she smiled and said to herself, "Are your ears burning Levi?" His message read:

"Want to go over to Piper's tomorrow together?"

"Sure"

"Hit a patio first? Going to be nice day."

"Love it"

"What are you up to now?"

"Writing. You?"

"Just left Barbara with some friends at a club downtown. Want some company? Or no? ...writing?"

"Company would be nice. Bourne is on TV at 10:00."

"Perfect, make the popcorn, be there in fifteen minutes."

Sadie saved her work and closed the lid, turned off the lights and went to her room to freshen up. She was giddy with excitement and looking forward to hanging out. She threw on a black, cotton cardigan over her white tank with yoga pants and

READ BETWEEN THE LINES

washed her face, piling her hair in a messy bun on the top of her head. Lastly she headed to the kitchen to pull out her air popcorn maker and kernels. She just finished making the first bowl when there was a knock at the door.

"Come in!" she said and heard Levi put the key in the door and enter.

"Smells good in here."

"Just about to make my bowl, here you go. Can you turn on the TV, I think it was on channel 575."

Levi grabbed his bowl and headed to the couch. Sadie brought them over a couple Radlers to drink. Settling in like an old married couple on the couch to watch their movie, both of them content and nowhere they would rather be.

"So you didn't want to stay with Barbara and her friends tonight?"

"No, not my scene. You know that."

"There were times it was," Sadie said confidently, thinking of what she was writing before he arrived.

"Depends on the company I am with," he said and winked at her. Sadie blushed and looked down at her popcorn. "Besides, it's a girl's night, I wasn't welcome."

29

"Ahhh, the truth comes out."

"What about you, why are you home, alone?"

"Levi. I am home most weekends alone." Sadie laughed. "You know me, I would rather write, have a quiet evening, and then every once in a blue moon let loose."

"Yes, so when you let loose, let me know. I like to be around for those."

"Ha! Well, there won't be one of those until I am done this book. Then we celebrate." She reached across the couch and held out her drink to cheers him. He obliged.

Sadie must have fallen asleep at some point during the movie. She woke with a blanket on her and Levi gone. A note was on the table. "Didn't want to wake you, will text you in the morning." Some movie date she was, she didn't remember getting through even half of the movie. Her late-night writing was catching up to her. Her watch said two in the morning. Squinting at the door to make sure it was locked, Sadie headed straight to bed.

Chapter 4

Piper's Party

They sat enjoying a cold beer with a basket of chips and guacamole. It was a beautiful Sunday afternoon. The patios in this part of the city were packed, the streets were full with people milling about, enjoying the latter part of the weekend. Sadie and Levi were taking advantage of the early summer warmth and talking about sailing. Levi couldn't wait to get back out on the water. He had a boat at the Scarborough Bluffs, just east of downtown Toronto.

"We should have gone there today."

"It's not in the water yet. I'm having a little work done to it, then I'm going to take it up to the cottage for Canada Day. I plan on spending a lot more time up there this summer."

She thought it was strange he didn't ask her to go up. She had spent every summer holiday there over the last seven years. Maybe he was assuming it was an open invitation. Or, he might just want a romantic weekend with Barbara. The waiter came and cleared their glasses and Levi took care of the bill. They were headed to a barbeque at Piper's. She had asked them both to come and it wasn't unusual for them to go together.

"Where is Barb today?" Sadie asked as she got into Levi's car.

"She went to a bridal shower for a friend. She was disappointed she couldn't come."

"Bridal shower eh? You know what that means right?"

"What?"

"You know, thinking of her own wedding…"

"Oh no, no, no, we are not that serious. She's the maid of honour and had to be there today."

READ BETWEEN THE LINES

"Doesn't matter, you know she is sitting there choosing her colours and flowers – hey let's pick out your fave when we grab Piper's hostess gift."

Levi was shaking his head side to side, over-exaggerating.

They bantered for a bit, went to the florist, and hit up the liquor store for wine. They pulled into Piper's driveway an hour later in an area of Toronto known as the Beach. She lived in a modern semi-detached home with a large deck and manicured backyard. It was times like these that Sadie thought about her apartment lifestyle and yearned for an outdoor space. She had grown up on an acre in the middle of farm fields. Friends always found it interesting that she now lived in the city and in a condo no less.

Sadie had gone to journalism school at Ryerson University, which is where she met Ally; they even roomed with each other for a year. They both had aspirations to be entertainment reporters. Sadie had written for a Toronto publication, which is when she met Samantha, but left after her first book went big and she was offered a book deal. Ally had a great gig working remotely out of her home, writing for various blogs, papers, and websites. She wanted to someday open up a business making and selling natural bath and body products using essential oils.

33

In the meantime Ally made products out of her home on the side that she sold online, and her friends ate them up, they smelled so good.

They walked up the steps to the front door. "Hey, so glad you guys could come!" Piper said as she ushered them in.

They had decided on a hostess gift together. Levi handed her a bottle of a nice red wine from Chile, and Sadie handed her a bouquet of pink dahlias.

"These are almost as gorgeous as you, Sadie! Thank you, guys! Come in, come in, everyone is out back. I think you know most people here, make yourself comfortable."

Sadie blushed at the compliment. Levi winked at her and put his hand at the small of her back to walk her into the backyard. The gesture took her by surprise causing her to take a deep breath. It was almost as though they were a real-life couple. For a moment, Sadie thought, as she had done so many times before, THIS is what it would be like.

Piper looked amazing as usual. Today she was wearing an emerald green maxi dress that clung in all the right places. She linked her arm with some gorgeous guy and whispered something in his ear, and then they both looked at each other and giggled.

READ BETWEEN THE LINES

Piper was simply vivacious and her backyard matched. It was beautiful; the space had literally been turned into an oasis. They made their way over to the edge of the deck, when Levi's phone rang. He excused himself to take the call, mouthing to her, "It's Barbara."

Sadie looked around to see if there were some familiar faces. A really good looking guy looked over at her at the same time. He mouthed "hi" as Piper was handing her a mojito. "This has your name on it, girl." Piper then clinked her own mint mojito against it. I'll introduce you to Mick later, he's a cutie." Sadie looked back and he was busy talking to a beautiful redhead. Everyone at this party looked like they walked off the runway. Certainly wasn't just a barbeque for authors, and she didn't know everyone as Piper had suggested. Pausing to take a sip of her drink, Piper asked, "How do you two do it?"

"What? Who?"

"You and Levi. You are both ridiculously gorgeous and yet keep it platonic; you've been friends and colleagues for years, how do you do it?"

"Ah." Sadie turned to look towards the garden doors as Levi was coming out and headed towards them.

"Another time." Piper said as her eyes glinted.

"Um yes," Sadie said as her face turned red again.

"What's up?" Levi asked her, "You're blushing. Is Piper giving you compliments again?" Levi teased.

"No, no, it's just from the mojito," Sadie said and bent to admire the pot of flowers at her feet to avoid looking at them.

"She doesn't know how beautiful she is, Piper, completely oblivious."

Piper's eyes widened and her mouth formed a huge, knowing smile. She winked at Sadie as she stood back up.

"Why she is single is beyond me."

"Well I know guys that would line up, Sadie," Piper offered.

"I love the colours you chose for your planters, Piper," Sadie said, ignoring both of them and changing the subject. Although she was thrilled to hear him say she was beautiful, she was freaking out and she was not prepared for this attention. She wasn't used to Levi talking like this. They flirted all the time, but it was different, he was looking at her different.

READ BETWEEN THE LINES

Piper could see that she was rattled and was kind enough to move on to talking about the flowers. Levi saw someone he knew and excused himself.

"Okay girl, there are some serious hints dropping over here!" Piper leaned in. "What are you waiting for, you two are perfect for each other!"

"It's complicated, Piper."

"How so?"

"Well, let's start with the fact he has a girlfriend! AND I don't want to get another agent any time soon."

"I don't see Barbara here, where is she?"

"She had plans today, for her friend's bridal shower, a perfectly acceptable excuse," Sadie confirmed.

"Well, I've never seen him look at Barbara the way he looks at you. It's not that serious."

"He still has a girlfriend and that's just not my style."

"Maybe he just needs a nudge?" Piper winked at Sadie. "Besides, I like everyone, but there is something about that girl that rubs me the wrong way."

"Yes, me too."

"All I'm saying is it wouldn't hurt to give him a hint, let him know you're feeling the same. And as far as needing a new agent, I don't see why you would need to."

"I don't know..."

"Don't be ridiculous!"

"Don't be ridiculous about what?" Levi asked. Piper and Sadie exchanged glances and Piper thought fast.

"Just telling Sadie her book will be another best seller. She has nothing to worry about." Sadie played along, shrugging her shoulders.

"Of course it will!" Levi exclaimed. "Hey Piper I haven't heard from Charles lately, is he still writing?"

"He's taken a sabbatical in France to visit family. He assures me that he'll be ready to get started when he gets back. I'll put him in touch with you, I know he's still looking for a literary agent."

"That's great, thanks."

"Sadie, I want to introduce you to my friend Mick. He's gorgeous and single. He's over here." Piper winked at her, and she knew that this was all

READ BETWEEN THE LINES

part of Piper's plan. According to Ally she had bets on them too after all.

Levi watched as Piper grabbed Sadie by the hand and led her to a group across from them. A tall, dark-haired guy smiled as they were introduced. He figured that was Mick. Hmph, he thought, looking down at his drink and swirling it before taking a large gulp. It hit him right in his gut; he was jealous. What right did he have to be jealous since he was in a relationship with Barbara? He was happy with her, things were going great. But yet here he was. His blood boiled at the sight of this guy ogling Sadie like that.

Feeling rather barbaric he wanted to walk over, wrap his arms around her waist, plant a kiss on her, and claim his woman. Not that Sadie was one to be "claimed"; an independent, free spirit since the first time they met, she didn't need a man.

Sadie was feisty, yet one of the nicest people he knew. She knew what she liked and always chased after her dreams. And she was stunning. He couldn't take his eyes off her. He hadn't been able to for the last seven years and somehow they had stayed in a platonic relationship. It was easy when she was new to the agency and he knew that they would frown upon it. Now his colleagues had running bets on when it would happen. It had been

39

JILL BREUGEM

easy when she was in relationships, because he wasn't that kind of guy to come between anyone. It had been easy when he was in his long term relationship with Marilyn, even though he knew that was doomed from the beginning. Reflecting, maybe it hadn't been that easy, it was just that he had a moral compass. Yet now here he was, his compass malfunctioning with no idea where to go. All he could think of was Sadie. It wasn't fair to Barbara.

And, before he knew it, he stood his athletic six foot frame up tall, walked over to where Piper left Sadie with Mick, put his arm around her waist, pulled her into a side embrace, kissed her on the cheek and gave Mick the "nod".

Chapter 5

Making Plans

A couple weeks had passed since she started to write about herself and Levi. She couldn't believe how easy it was to write their love story; the words just came to life so easily. Their friendship included one favourite memory after another, and she shared all the details, embellishing where she wanted.

Unfortunately she was having writer's block with the "backup" novel. The story wasn't quite coming together, so she focused whatever time she had to writing it. She wrote all morning until Levi showed up for his usual lunch date. He was so odd at Piper's barbeque, speaking and acting like never before. Could he possibly feel the same as her?

"What are your plans for Canada Day? Want to head up to my cottage for a little R&R?" Levi asked as he stole a piece of tempeh from her plate. The stat holiday was still a couple weeks away and she was wondering if and when he would ask.

She slipped off her stool and went to the fridge to pour some milk into her mug, grabbed a tea bag and pressed the kettle's lever down to boil. Her hair was in a messy bun and she was wearing jean shorts and a white tank top. She didn't need to do more than this, she was so beautiful he thought to himself. She didn't need a stitch of makeup. She didn't need to spend hours getting ready like Barbara would. She was perfect. He adjusted in his seat, and took a long drink of water. She had no idea the effect she had on him. She leaned on her elbows in front of him and answered, "I would love to."

"Perfect, when can you head up? I have a meeting with the Boyle sisters about their cookbook on the thirtieth at 10:00, after that I am good to go." He paused, "Hey, ask Ally if she wants to join us, and I can see if Oliver wants to come" he said. A blond curl broke free from behind his ear. Sadie loved his full head of hair; she dreamt of grabbing fistfuls all the time.

READ BETWEEN THE LINES

"So when do you want me to stop by?" he said as he pushed the curl back behind his ear, interrupting her from her thoughts.

"Come grab me after lunch. I've been staying up late writing and sleeping-in these days. I have a good groove going on, I want to keep it up so that I can get my agent off my back" Sadie said with a wink. "I'll probably bring my laptop up to the cottage, in case the mood inspires me there as well." She said, "Oh, and Ally is going up to Gage's cabin."

"Is it getting serious?" he asked his left eyebrow raising.

"It looks like it is" Sadie answered. Sadie knew that he had wanted to set up his best friend Oliver with Ally since he was moving back to Toronto. Oliver met Ally years ago and was completely smitten, but at the time he was moving to London, England for his job and didn't pursue it. Sadie shared the interest with Ally after Levi had told her one night over beers at her apartment.

"Oh ya, he adores her," Levi had said. "If he wasn't moving to London he would have asked her out on the spot." And Ally would have accepted she thought to herself. After meeting Oliver, Ally had grabbed her by the arm and pulled her into the powder room to ask, "What's his story? I think I'm

43

in love." to which Sadie shared that he was moving away.

Levi stood waiting for her response about Ally's current boyfriend Gage.

"I've only met him once. They spend a lot of time together these days, but I guess that's what happens."

"Do you think its love already?"

Sadie felt the heat rush into her cheeks and turned from him so he wouldn't see and busied herself with some dishes in the sink.

"Oh, I think sometimes you just know," Sadie said and continued, "Or maybe that is just the romance author in me talking." She turned back to him, shrugging and smiled.

"Well, either way, she will be missed at the cottage, always fun when you two get together." He paused. "Although I think you should take a much-deserved break on our nation's holiday, I don't want to get between you and your groove with the book," Levi said with a smirk and winked back at her. He held her gaze, while tapping the counter, and then placed his hands on his lap. Why was he so fidgety? They continued looking at each other for what seemed like a long time. What did she see in his eyes? It was like the other day when he stopped by

44

with the flowers. He looked like he had something to say. His phone interrupted their moment with a vibration. It was the fifth time since he arrived, and he continued to ignore it.

"Are you going to answer that?"

"It's Barb. She knows I'm here, I talked to her just before coming." He sounded irritated. He pushed the phone away from him and loaded his dishes in the dishwasher.

"Maybe she has something urgent to tell you," she said sarcastically, trying to get out of his way.

"I doubt it," he countered. Sadie startled when he reached for something on the counter behind her. His arm left instant goosebumps where it had brushed against hers. She changed her footing and took a deep breath, rubbing her arm to get rid of the evidence. He grabbed her empty mug and spoon and put them away.

"You know you're just going to make her hate me even more," Sadie stated.

"She doesn't hate you, Sadie," he said as he closed the dishwasher and grabbed his keys. "She just likes to have me all to herself, and to be honest, it's growing old. Thanks for lunch Sade, I gotta jet."

That was the best news Sadie had heard all day. She could only hope that he would see the light soon because she didn't know how much more she could take of Babs. She didn't know what he saw in her. Yes, she was pretty in her own way. Barbara had auburn hair that was always blown out to perfection, her face was attractive, she had very classic and expensive taste in clothing, but her personality was less than desirable. And it wasn't just because she was in love with Levi; Barbara was simply not a nice person. She knew Barbara hated that Sadie and Levi were close and spent as much time as they did together. And she would probably feel the same if her boyfriend had a close friend that was a girl. She wasn't immune to insecurity and jealousy.

Sadie broke up with Ethan a few months ago. He didn't have girls that were his friends, but he worked with a lot of women, and Sadie witnessed them falling all over him. Like most men, he loved the attention he got. It used to drive her crazy because she wasn't one to get jealous, and it turned her into someone she didn't like. It took her a long time to get comfortable in her own skin and now that she was, she hated feeling insecure. And what was worse, was that Ethan seemed to like making her feel that way, it was a way of keeping her in her place.

READ BETWEEN THE LINES

In the end, they weren't a good match. She hated feeling insecure and lonely, and needed more emotionally from him. And she had to admit that she did compare him to Levi all the time. Conversation flowed freely with Levi; they had common interests, likes, and dislikes. Ethan and Sadie didn't see eye to eye on politics, her volunteer work, or how she ate. She never understood why people had such a hard time with her being a vegetarian. It wasn't hurting them, and she never expected anyone to change how they ate to suit her. The fact that he saw volunteer work as a waste of time just drove her spare. It reminded her of a saying: "Live for the cause, not for the applause". Ethan couldn't do anything without the applause of benefit to him in some form of monetary value. He had everything handed to him. He was fed with a silver spoon, educated at the finest schools, and grew up with entitlement. It didn't matter how nice he was to Sadie; the way he treated everyone and everything else was a direct reflection of the person he truly was. She could not continue a relationship with someone who felt so strongly, passionately, and differently from her.

She locked the door after Levi left, and got ready to head out for the afternoon. She had some research to do on her other book and wanted to get out of the house before her cleaner Jenny arrived.

JILL BREUGEM

She left the payment on the kitchen counter, grabbed her phone, a notepad and pen, threw it all in her bag, and headed out.

Chapter 6

Coffee Shop

Sadie's wrist buzzed with a text from Ally. "Meet me at Starbucks at two." She had almost forgotten their plans to meet up.

Sadie threw her phone in her brown hobo bag, pulled it over her body, slipped on her sandals, and headed out. When she hit the street, she put her aviators on and walked the five minutes to the coffee shop. She could see through the window that Ally was already sitting at a table, waiting for her with their drinks, Ally got a caramel macchiato and Sadie a chai tea latte. Even though it was a warm day, they enjoyed their hot drinks. Just as she grabbed the door, someone was coming out at the same time, causing them to collide. Icy liquid splashed everywhere, on her chest, neck and even up her nose! Licking her lips she tasted iced frappuccino.

"Oh my god, I'm so sorry!" they said in unison. Sadie looked up into beautiful brown eyes. He had short brown hair, a chiseled jaw and was wearing a very expensive tapered suit. He was gorgeous. Just then it hit her, her face flushed as she realized it was Mick from Piper's party!

"I'm so sorry, let me buy you a new one", Sadie said. "And give me your dry cleaning bill. " Eyeing his expensive suit, she went to grab napkins. She handed him a pile and grabbed a handful for herself, but sadly there was no helping either of them. She wiped at her nose imagining what a sight that was! And thankfully, she had a small cardigan around her waist, worn in case she was cold in just her tank top in the shop.

"No, no, it was my fault, I wasn't looking up," he said, "I have another suit in the office. Can I buy you a coffee?" he asked.

"Thank you, but I'm meeting a friend," Sadie said as she motioned towards Ally, who was nearby, waving and smiling. "She'll take a rain check though!" Ally blurted. Sadie quickly glared at her friend and then back up into those brown eyes. He was very attractive.

"Sadie?"

"Yes. Mick, right?" This was so embarrassing, Piper is going to be mortified she thought while frappuccino dripped out of her nose.

He opened his wallet, grabbed a business card and handed it to her. "Rain check on the coffee?" He said warmly.

"Thank you," she said and smiled.

"I'm glad I ran into you Sadie". They said goodbye and she went over to the table where Ally was waiting to pounce.

"Sadie! He is gorgeous! Only you would run into a guy, spill his drink all over his Brioni suit, and get asked out!"

"Ally! You know I'm not interested, I just told you about Levi!" She dropped the card on the table.

"Yes and last I heard he has a girlfriend. At least go have some fun with yummy guy until Levi is single."

"Sadie just shook her head at her best friend and took a sip of her favorite drink. "Sadie, you saw him right?" said Ally picking up the card. "You SAW Mick? He even has a cool name to match the hotness. And he was so into you. He couldn't take his eyes off of you!"

"He's not my type, reminds me of Ethan," Sadie retorted.

"No way, don't you dare compare him to that conceited, no emotion robot!" Ally was always right to the point. It was one of the things Sadie loved about her.

"I met him last week at Piper's! So embarrassing."

"Don't be, was just as much his fault. What do you mean you met last week?! Spill it Sade!"

"Nothing much, Piper introduced us, we talked for a bit. But then this strange thing happened with Levi, I think Mick might have gotten the impression that we were dating."

"What did Levi do?"

Sadie hesitated and then said, "He came over and put his arm around my waist, pulled me into his side, he even kissed me on the cheek." She looked down at her hands, feeling her face blush (why did it always give her away?). Looking back up she said, "He definitely gave Mick a hint."

"How dare he?! You're single, he's not! He can't have you both. "

READ BETWEEN THE LINES

"I know. It surprised me too. But it also made me happy." She shrugged.

"You need to go out with Mick and show Levi that you aren't just going to be sitting back while he dates whoever he wants!"

"I'll think about it"

"You bet you're going to think about it!" Ally took Sadie's phone from the table and entered his phone number into her phone. "There. Hunky Mick is saved."

"You're hilarious!" Sadie grabbed her phone and threw it in her purse as they both giggled.

Sadie and Ally visited for a couple hours. They talked more about the dashing stranger and how funny it had been. She could be such a big klutz, "Only you Sadie," Ally said. They talked more about the feelings she had for Levi, and why Sadie had held back on saying anything for so long.

"I'm your best friend, why didn't you say something before?"

"I was just scared that once I put it out there, it's out there."

"And what is wrong with that?"

"What if he doesn't feel the same, or he does and we ruin everything."

"Don't think that's possible, but since he has a girlfriend, you could definitely have some fun with Hunky Mick in the meantime." She was relentless.

They also talked about Ally's new boyfriend Gage. Things were getting serious and Ally was happy. She beamed when she spoke of him. It sounded like he was crazy about her too. Ally was simply giddy talking about heading up to Gage's cabin. Sadie didn't even bother to mention the option to go to Levi's. She knew Ally was one hundred percent committed to heading up to Gage's.

"Can't wait, Sade!"

"That's amazing. What's it been, a few months now?"

"Yep."

"Have you met his family yet?"

"No." Ally shifted in her seat. "We haven't talked about his family much. I get the feeling they might not get along very well, he gets a little funny when I bring them up."

"Oh," I answered wondering what that was all about. "Well, where's his cottage?"

"Near Minden. I should get home and back home," Ally said. "I've left my mom there to help

READ BETWEEN THE LINES

with some online orders. She is bound to mix something up." Ally liked to poke fun at her mom Catriona helping her at the essential oil home based business, but they both knew how much her mom meant to her. It had been Ally and her mom all of her life; they were soul sisters. They even looked just like each other. The same petite (but feisty), athletic build, with thick ginger curls. Their cherub faces both had a sprinkling of freckles which flattered their youthful appearances. They were both knockouts, and often mistaken for sisters.

Ally's dad was a famous ball player. Her parents had met when her mom was waitressing at a restaurant that he used to frequent when in town. He was drawn to her green eyes, attitude and Irish accent. He was handsome and charming. They were magnetic together. Although the chemistry and mutual respect was there, he was busy on the road and at that time, not ready to settle down or trade in his lifestyle. He loved her, but not enough to stay.

As a result, sadly he didn't play a huge role in Ally's life. He would call once a month or so and come to visit once a year. But that was as far as it went. She knew he took care of her mom and paid child support over the years. Her mom said that she didn't need such a large sum of money each month, but he insisted. Catriona put away the money away for her daughter's education and to help Ally purchase her first home. Catriona had dated here and there, but had never found that special someone. Ally knew that as long as her dad showed up once a year her mom never would.

Finishing off their drinks, Sadie and Ally hugged and went their separate ways, knowing it would literally be minutes before one of them texted each other again.

Chapter 7

Road Trip

The next day when Sadie locked up her penthouse apartment, she had a bounce in her step. She was so excited about spending these next few days with Levi. They hadn't been alone for more than a couple hours in quite a while; she longed to spend some time with him. They went up to the cottage a couple years ago on their own, and spent the weekend swimming, canoeing, sailing, and in front of the campfire. It was one of the best times she can remember.

She tossed her keys in her bag, grabbed her backpack, her laptop bag and practically ran to the elevator. The elation came to a grinding halt when she saw Barbara sitting in the front seat of his car. She had no idea she was going to be the third wheel. But she should have known when he asked if Ally wanted to join them, and she should have known he would be inviting his girlfriend of six months. Her stomach churned.

Levi grabbed her bags and put them in the trunk before she could object. Closing the trunk he gave her a half smile, knowing what she was thinking.

"Levi ...I can head up to my parents, stay back and write..." her voice trailed off.

"Come on now, it will be fun! I want my girls to get to know each other better."

Sadie rolled her eyes as she squeaked "Great" before climbing into the back seat. His girls? What the hell?

"Hi Barbara, how are you?"

"Oh I'm good, Sadie. Surprised you wanted to come with us since Ally and Oliver couldn't..."

Barbara was saying exactly what Sadie was feeling. She was such a cow. Even if she was thinking it, she was so rude.

"We're going to have a great time," Levi interjected. "I plan on getting the sailboat out. We can go for a canoe, call a few friends up there, have a bonfire, do some fireworks, and have a bit of a party on Canada Day. So I was thinking of making pasta tonight with a salad," Levi rattled on, trying to change the subject.

"Oh, you know I am not doing carbs, baby," Barbara whined. Sadie's eyes rolled again. She had a feeling she'd be doing a lot of that the next few days. "How can I keep this figure you love so much if I eat carbs?" Barbara continued.

Sadie looked at Levi in the rear view mirror and gave him a wink and a smirk.

Levi avoided Barbara's comment and quickly moved on to say, "There will be lots of salad and we can always barbeque you up some chicken if you want?"

Barbara put her hand on his neck and sighed, "Sure baby, whatever." Her nails were like talons, long and pointy making their mark on his skin just for Sadie to see. Ugh, Sadie thought, THREE days. He was going to owe her for this.

'Sure baby, whatever', Sadie mouthed to Levi who was looking at her in the rear-view mirror. His eyes opened wider and she could see the colour changing in his face to a soft pink. His blue eyes shifted to the road. She closed her eyes and reopened them to find him looking at her again. Darting his eyes back to the road, he knew he had been caught. Sadie closed her eyes the rest of the way, daydreaming things were very different heading up to the cottage.

When they arrived, Barbara hopped out of the car and walked to the cottage with only her purse in tow. With her mouth agape, Sadie looked at Levi. He shrugged. Sadie sighed and helped Levi bring everything into the log style cabin, making several trips while Barbara sat on the couch scrolling through her phone. She was so annoying. Three days! He would so owe her for this.

"Thanks, Sadie," he said, looking at her with appreciation. He continued to follow Sadie to her room and whispered, "I know you think she is a little high maintenance, maybe she is, but she can be really nice too Sadie. Hopefully you two can get to know each other better?"

He wasn't even sure why he was saying this. Well he did know. He was testing the waters, he wanted to see her reaction, wanted a sign, something. It had been seven amazing years of friendship, but he wanted more. He had known for a long time.

"Sure, Levi," Sadie said and took the bags from his hands. She turned her back to him for a moment, opened one of her bags on the bed, and pulled out her laptop. "I'm going to head down to the dock and write."

Levi stepped out of her way. There was nothing else Sadie could say. She wasn't going to promise him anything when it came to Barbara.

Chapter 8

Cottage

"Levi, it's hot in here, you said there was an air conditioner, I don't feel it," Barbara whined as the door closed behind Sadie. Good riddance for now she thought. There was no way on this hot humid day Barbara would make her way to the lake. She was safe there.

Sadie made her way down the path towards the lake. She loved it here. She had been coming to Levi's cottage since he bought it, a purchase he made after signing Sadie on as a client. She came with him to look at property in the Muskoka and they both fell in love. It was a beautiful log-cabin style cottage with large windows facing the water, a wrap-around deck, and a path through the tall pines that leading down to a boathouse, dock and the glorious lake. Sadie grabbed a cold beer from the boathouse fridge, and settled herself into a big lounger on the dock.

The sun was warm but the air was clear. The lake looked like glass. She slipped on her ear buds and put on some Chris Stapleton. She took a long sip of her beer and closed her eyes. She was here for three days. How would she deal with being the third wheel for three days? This was going to be painful, she should have driven up by herself and feigned illness. She grabbed her phone and started to text Ally.

"Hey Sadie, want some company?" Levi interrupted her thoughts, and pulled a chair over.

Sadie jumped, and pulled out her earplugs, clearing the private text she was in the process of writing. "Sure, of course." Pausing she dared to ask, "Where's Barbara?"

"She has a headache and is having a nap before dinner." He opened his beer, and leaned over to cheers her.

"Are you cheersing her headache, the nap or…" she smirked

READ BETWEEN THE LINES

"Just you, I'm just cheersing you," he said with sincerity.

"Ah…" They clinked their beers together, followed by big gulps.

"Hey, let's take the canoe out." Levi suggested.

"Are you sure? Barbara won't be looking for you?"

"Don't be silly, she just took some horse pill, she's out for a while. Wait here. Hold this. "He passed her his beer and went off to the boathouse. A few minutes later he appeared with the canoe over his head and sat it down on the dock. Sadie watched him, mesmerized. How he kept that build doing very little was unfair to the male population. She had always been a fan of his broad shoulders and strong arms, so much so that she wondered what it would be like to be carried away in them. Her arms around his neck, her head resting on his chest…

"Sadie?" He said looking at her like he had said her name several times.

"Oh sorry, was just thinking of something for the book," she responded, feeling her face flush, and hoping to heaven she hadn't said anything out loud.

He passed her a life jacket and a paddle, pushed the canoe into the water, and stepped in. He held onto the dock and helped her in. She was not as

65

steady getting in, in fact he had to hold onto the dock with two hands before they not only went shooting out into the lake ill prepared, they would have tipped. Sadie squealed and sat down quickly, giggling to herself while Levi just laughed and shook his head. "Every time, Sadie." Taking one big gulp of his beer, he finished it and left it on the dock. He sat down and used his paddle to push away from the dock.

The lake was beautiful, it looked like glass, and it was a perfect day to go for a canoe ride. They stayed close to the shore, taking their usual route. How many times had they gone out in the canoe over the years, sharing their dreams and fears, like best friends do. Sadie was sure today would be no different, enjoying the sounds of the water gently lapping around the base and listening to the birds overhead. The smell of freshwater and forest tickled her nose. She closed her eyes, feeling the warmth of the sun on her face, enjoying what Mother Nature was doing to her senses.

"Barbara. She is a good woman. I hope you will have an opportunity to see that at some point this long weekend." He spoke as if he was trying to convince himself.

"Ah…" Sadie said. Is this what we are talking about today? She'd rather chew sand on the beach.

READ BETWEEN THE LINES

She didn't want to be like this, she didn't want to seem bitchy, but Barbara brought it out in her. She couldn't help herself, and he was blind to it. She loved him, and yes she wanted more than friendship, but she also didn't want to lose her friendship with him over this.

"Don't worry, Levi, lots of time yet this weekend," she said over her shoulder.

"Why don't you like her, Sadie?"

"Who said I didn't like her?" She turned the questioning on him.

He set the paddle across his lap, leaving Sadie to steer alone at the water's edge. He waited until their eyes met and then he asked her again, "Why?"

She paused for what seemed like eternity, considering how this conversation could go if she wanted it to. She had a few choices. One - Tell him exactly how she was feeling about him. Two - Tell him exactly how she felt about Barbara or Three - Suck it up and say something nice.

Just then Sadie realized she had steered them into a rocky shore and panicked. She pushed out with her paddle with force, but all it did was rock the canoe side to side. "Hold on Sadie!" he said as he put his paddle in to try to assist. But it was too late. Sadie had made a spastic movement that sent

67

the canoe over and both of them in the cool water. She heard him yell her name one more time as the water went over her head. Arms and legs were flailing, heads bobbing and she couldn't help but laugh.

"Are you okay?" he asked as they caught their bearings. She nodded. "Why do I take you out in the canoe? Wasn't up for a swim yet," he teased. Sadie smiled and looked at him apologetically, trying to contain her laughter. He started to laugh too, knowing what a klutz she could be. "How many years have we canoed? You do this to me at least once a summer!"

"Think of it this way, you're good now for the season," she retorted with a wink. They swam over to a shallow area, Levi pulling the canoe along with him. Once there, they climbed out of the water and back into the canoe. Sadie giggled the whole way back and he never brought up Barbara again. He would just look at her shake his head and start laughing. Her scheme to not talk about Barbara worked she giggled to herself, knowing full well that the canoe dumping was not intentional or planned.

When they got back to the dock they sat again on the chairs drying off from their adventure, laughing and enjoying another beer when Sadie's

READ BETWEEN THE LINES

phone went off. The phone was sitting on the dock between the two of them, Levi picked it up, looked at the screen and handed it to her.

"Hunky Mick?" he said frowning with his eyebrows raised.

Mortified, Sadie took the phone from him.

"Hello," Sadie got up and walked away from Levi on the dock.

"Hi Sadie, its Mick from the coffee shop, and uh...Piper's."

"Hi Mick, how are you?" she paused, "how did you get my number?"

"I knew you would be wondering that...I ran into Ally there this morning, she gave it to me. She said you might not call me, and asked me to ask you not to be too mad at her." He laughed.

That Ally...boy, she was going to text her when they got off the phone!

"She did, did she?"

"She mentioned you were away for the weekend, but I was hoping that next week I could take you for dinner. Have you been to Bailey's on a Thursday night?"

69

"No, I haven't," Sadie admitted. She had always wanted to go and check out the Indie bands they showcased on Thursdays.

"I would love to take you, if you're up for it?" He sounded so pleasant, and she remembered those brown eyes. Looking up at the cottage and back at Levi, she thought of Barbara and the conversation she had with Ally.

"That sounds great, Mick. I'm looking forward to it."

"Great, I'll pick you up at 7:30, call or text me if anything changes"

They said goodbye and Sadie headed back to the dock.

She sat down, and Levi asked again, "Hunky Mick?"

Sadie explained how they met him at Piper's and how they ran into each other at the coffee shop, and how Ally had saved the number. She left out how he had been part of the conversation, and ultimately why Ally pushed the idea of dating Mick.

"Did he call to ask you out?"

"Yes we're going to go out on Thursday to Bailey's on the Esplanade."

READ BETWEEN THE LINES

"Oh that's great, great place." Levi looked down at his beer, he looked like he was about to say something, and then got up from his chair and headed toward the cottage.

"Where are you going?" she asked him.

"I'm going to head up and take a shower. Dinner will be around 7:00, okay?"

"Okay." She watched him walk back up, confused by his change in mood.

What the hell was that? He brought his girlfriend to the cottage, talked to me about her being a good woman, but had the nerve to look and act jealous about her date with Mick? Men were impossible, she thought as she drank the rest of her beer and opened her laptop to write.

Chapter 9

Barbara

Levi knew he had to end things with Barbara and tell Sadie how he really felt. He felt terrible stringing Barbara along like this, knowing that his heart and head were with the beautiful blonde sitting down on his dock right now. He was enjoying himself, until that Mick guy called. Who did he think he was? I made it pretty clear at Piper's. Guys had a code, and I delivered it. But then he called and not only did Sadie sound happy to hear from him, she was headed out on a date with him.

JILL BREUGEM

He tiptoed around the cottage, not wanting to wake up Barbara, and headed into the shower. When he got out Barbara was there waiting for him.

"What are you doing?" she asked.

"Having a shower."

"Why?" she asked, tapping her foot. She looked accusing and mad.

"I fell in the lake, well we both did. It was funny..."

"You both did?" Barbara interrupted.

"Yes, went for a canoe and it never fails..."he was laughing and his voice trailed off when he realized that Barbara was not finding it very funny.

"Hmph. How nice."

"What's the problem, Barb?" He didn't like her tone, when he did nothing wrong.

"Nothing," she said and turned on her heel. He followed her out with a towel around his waist. She headed into the bedroom. Hearing a noise behind him, he turned. Sadie was getting a bottle of water.

Wow. Wow. Wow. She was trying not to look, but couldn't help herself, even with him catching her in the act. She simply could not avert her eyes.

READ BETWEEN THE LINES

She started to giggle. Levi was standing there, towel around his waist.

"Hi. If you need to get in the shower, go ahead, I'm done in there." He said.

"Yep." she said, raising one eyebrow, still unable to move her eyes.

"I have to go talk to Barbara," he motioned towards the bedroom.

"Sure thing," Sadie answered still staring.

"Okay," he said and headed into the bedroom to speak to Barbara. If he didn't smooth things over it was going to be a long few days up here. He knew he probably should dial things back with Barbara, perhaps even end things, but he wasn't about to do it up here, especially now since Sadie was headed out on a date with "Hunky Mick".

When Levi walked into the bedroom, Barbara was packing her bag.

"What's up, Barbara? What are you doing?" he asked, his tone firm.

"You're taking me home!" She yelled.

"Why?"

"You know why," she said, stomping around the room.

"No, I don't know why," he answered frankly, sitting on the edge of the bed.

"Well, I think three's a crowd."

"Barbara, if anyone would be feeling that way right now, it's Sadie, "he assured her.

"Oh really yet, YOU, needed a shower."

"I told you we fell in the water. We fell out of the canoe."

"Mmm hmm." She wasn't looking at him.

"Barbara, I am telling you the truth, nothing happened." Levi said as he grabbed clothes from his dresser. As much as he knew that the end was near for this relationship, he didn't like being accused when he had done nothing wrong, yet. "You know Sadie and I have been friends for years." Thinking of 'Hunky Mick', he continued, "And will continue to be friends for years to come, but that is all." He went over to her, feeling bad for making her feel this way when clearly Sadie and he were always going to be just friends.

Putting his arm around her waist he pulled her in. She reluctantly let him. Running her hands on his chest and up over his shoulders, she said, "I don't want to be made a fool of, Levi."

READ BETWEEN THE LINES

"And you have nothing to worry about. Nothing. Okay?" He pulled her closer and kissed her.

"Okay."

"I'm going to get dressed and then I'll pour us some wine and start dinner. Sound good?"

"I know something that sounds even better." She teased in his ear and kicked the door close with her foot.

Chapter 10

Splash

That night after dinner, Sadie turned into her room early, having gotten a little too much sun on the lake during the day. In the room sat a queen size wrought iron bed, with piles of pillows and quilts made with love by Levi's grandmother. Beside the bed sat a simple antique side table and lamp, and at the foot of the bed a matching dresser. There was a welcome breeze coming in the window, blowing the sheer white curtains beside the bed.

She brought a bottle of wine with her into her room and settled in to catch up on a little social media. She liked to reach out to her fans through

Facebook, Twitter and Instagram, read their feedback, and connect. She thought it was important to stay in touch as they had indeed given her so much in her short writing career.

She poured herself a healthy glass of wine and started to think again about Levi's reaction to Mick. Was she dreaming it, overthinking it? He acted similarly at Piper's. He seemed to always be justifying his relationship with Barbara and what a nice person she was. She didn't know what that was all about. Why did he care what she thought of Barbara? Levi and Sadie were best friends, obviously it mattered to him what she thought about his girlfriends. But, it never seemed to matter in the past. He really seemed to be pushing this relationship with Sadie.

Her stomach turned at the thought. Was he looking for her permission? Was Levi getting that serious with her that it would make a difference if she liked her or not?

Maybe she did need to move on, as Ally suggested. The thought of her career and needing a new agent also loomed in her thoughts. She shook her head and took a gulp of wine. Focus.

She answered some fan's notes, re-tweeted a pile of comments and posted pictures of the lake to Instagram for her fans to see. Time marched on, and

READ BETWEEN THE LINES

when she looked at the clock it was midnight. She also had finished the whole bottle of wine. She knew this was going to hurt in the morning. Wine hangovers were the worst. She giggled and reached for her bag knowing that she had put a bottle of water in there earlier. That should help the cause. She giggled again.

Just then she heard the unthinkable. They must have gone to bed a little while ago, and proceeded to do what she had never wanted to hear. Worse than a wailing cat, why was she so loud? Did she want Sadie to hear? She was definitely making strange noises on purpose. They were at the other end of the cottage. She put some music on and put her earbuds in to try to drown out the noise. Then she started to sing a long, hoping that maybe they would get the hint that she was still awake. That didn't work.

Sadie threw her pillow over her head. It was making her very uncomfortable and jealous as heck. She couldn't breathe. Her heart started to race and she was feeling hot and nauseous. Was it the wine? She really thought she was going to be sick. She had to get out of the cottage, immediately. She didn't know where she was going to go once she went outside, anywhere but here. She jumped up, and knocked the nightstand. The empty bottle of wine and her glass went crashing to the floor. "Crap!" she exclaimed. She froze and thought about cleaning it up but thought better of it and kept going.

She ran out of her room and headed for the side door.

"Sadie? Sadie?" Levi opened his bedroom door, but she flew out of the cottage, and was headed for the water. Where the heck was she going? Ignoring Barbara's requests to leave Sadie alone, Levi chased after her. He heard a crash in her room and she was running frantically, he needed to know what was going on. Besides that, Barbara's joking around while making stupid sounds was getting on his nerves. He told her he was not in the mood.

Pushing past the branches, Sadie hurried down to the water. It was a dark night and the moon was only a sliver in the clear sky, but she had travelled this path a million times over the years.

What was she doing? Where was she going once she got down there? Levi thought. "Sadie!" he called after her. She passed the boathouse and continued to the water.

Sadie felt a sharp pain in her foot. She thought she heard Levi call to her, but she kept going. With no more thoughts, she jumped.

READ BETWEEN THE LINES

Pitch black. She opened her eyes. Nothing. She couldn't even see her hand in front of her face. The water was cool and the weeds were grabbing at her ankles. She gasped for air as she sprung to the surface. Panicking, she started to flail her arms and splash about. She felt an arm grab her around the waist, pull her and lift her out of the water. She was placed on the edge of the dock.

Levi pushed himself up out of the water onto the deck in a one swift movement. Bending over he put his hands on his knees, tried to catch his breath, while water dripped off of every inch of him.

"What...the...hell...Sadie," struggling to catch his breath and spit the words out. She opened her mouth, but nothing. What had she been thinking? What was she expecting to happen? She could have seriously hurt herself, or worse.

She was embarrassed. How was she going to explain this? What could she possibly say other than she had been overwhelmed, thought she was going to vomit, and couldn't listen to it anymore and ran and jumped in the lake? She groaned.

"Levi, what is going on?!" Barbara yelled from above.

"I'll be up in a minute!" Levi yelled up to the cottage.

JILL BREUGEM

"Levi!" she continued to yell.

"Go back inside!" Levi called.

Sadie stood up, her cotton tank and shorts clinging to her, and he noticed.

"I'm sorry, you shouldn't have followed me, and I just wasn't feeling well." Hiccupping she continued, "I needed air. Had too much wine," she said hiccupping again.

"I shouldn't have followed? I shouldn't have followed? You couldn't swim!" he hissed.

Sadie stumbled back but caught her footing.

"Had too much wine? Are you drunk?" he asked.

"I had a little wine." She giggled and said shhh to herself and giggled some more.

"Why are you giggling?" He ran his hands through his hair, grabbed her by the elbow and led her towards the cottage. "It's not funny Sadie, you freaked me out. You could have seriously hurt yourself or worse."

Sadie couldn't help herself. She started laughing and couldn't stop. Her laugh danced around the lake and back to the cottage. Her foot was throbbing, she was limping and must have stepped on a stick on the run down to the lake.

READ BETWEEN THE LINES

"Shhh, Sadie," he started to laugh himself. "I can't believe you just did that!"

They got to the cottage and Barbara was waiting for them inside.

"Someone's bleeding!!" Barbara shrieked.

Levi frantically started to search the cottage and found the broken glass in Sadie's room, came back and checked her feet and found that indeed one foot was cut, pretty bad.

"Sit down on the stool. You've cut your foot," he ordered, "I'll get the first aid kit."

Sadie did as she was told and looked down at her lap. As she started to look back up, she could feel Barbara glaring at her. She didn't want to give her the satisfaction and continued to look anywhere but in her direction. Sadie was trying hard to act sober and in control on the stool, sitting up straighter. Eventually Barbara stomped back into their room and slammed the door. Levi didn't even flinch, although they both knew he would pay for this somehow.

Levi returned and pulled up a stool in front of her, and put her leg across his lap. He turned her foot to inspect it. The cuts were on the pad of her foot and there was still some small shards sticking out like slivers. He gently wiped the blood with a

85

warm cloth, and picked the glass out. He took his time and Sadie watched him intently. Although she was injured and in pain, the sight of his strong hands holding her leg and foot took her mind off of it. He applied an ointment and wound gauze around her foot. He ran his hand up her smooth leg, to the back of her calf to lift her leg off his lap, and she got instant goosebumps. He saw and gave her leg a rub.

"Thank you, Levi."

He smiled at her warmly.

"Anything for you," adding, "but can we stay out of the water for the rest of the day?"

He stood up and went to the closet to get a broom and pan to clean up the broken wine bottle she had left in her wake. She had no idea it had broken, she was just so hell bent on getting out of there. Now she was feeling silly, and embarrassed.

"Are you done, Levi?" Barbara asked from their room.

Sadie hopped off the stool and said, "You go on, I'll clean it up, it was my fault." She limped towards him and he shook his head as she followed him to her room.

"Go on and change, you're in no state to clean it up limping and drunk. I will be there in a minute, Barb!"

READ BETWEEN THE LINES

Sadie grabbed a new tank top and pair of cotton shorts, went to the washroom to change, and returned a few minutes later to find him still gathering tiny shards from every corner of the room.

She laid across her bed on top of the covers. "I'm sorry, Levi," she mumbled, closed her eyes and drifted off to sleep.

Chapter 11

Going Home

The next day they headed home early. It was Canada Day and they would be missing out on the celebrations and fireworks, but Barbara apparently couldn't shake her headache, and Sadie was definitely ready to leave. At some point after cleaning up the wine bottle in her room Levi had covered her with a blanket. She slept in the next day and felt surprisingly good, except when she went to get out of bed and stepped down; her foot reminded her of the events the night before.

They packed up almost immediately and headed home. No one said a word, even Barbara

JILL BREUGEM

who usually had SOMETHING to say, was eerily quiet. Sadie appreciated the silence, and thanked Levi when they got to her apartment, assuring him she did not need help getting her things from the trunk, waving goodbye as she hurriedly limped into her building. Jones was there holding the door for her, "Back so soon, Sadie?"

Sadie gave him a half smile as they walked to the elevator. He was trying to take her bags for her, noticing that she was limping. "Do you need help with your things? Let me get that for you Sadie."

"No thank you, Jones, I got it."

"Not sure what Levi sees in that one out there, Sadie."

"Mmmhmm. Me neither." She shrugged and got on the elevator. She faced Jones and gave him a wave as the doors closed. Jones turned on his heel and headed back to doors, watching Levi drive away.

"Fool," he said to himself.

Jones was protective of Sadie. She reminded him of his own daughter that he hadn't seen for a long time due to a misunderstanding. Jones and his wife had separated years ago and she had told the children some sort of lies that kept them from

90

keeping up a relationship with him. He tried, and he tried again. He wouldn't give up.

Other than texting Ally to tell her the weekend was a bust, Sadie had no contact with anyone on Canada Day, and she was perfectly happy and disconnected at the same time. Like a leading lady in a romantic chick flick movie, Sadie had a long hot bubble bath, climbed into bed with the movie 'When Harry Met Sally', and a pint of ice cream.

When she woke the next day she decided that the best thing for her would be a visit to her parents. They always had a way of making her feel better, and she was missing them terribly right now. Their family home would always be her home.

Sadie hopped into her car and set her radio to her favourite country playlist. She took the long way so she would hit the back roads. Although it would take her longer to get there it was so much more enjoyable. When she hit the dirt roads ten minutes from her parents' home, her heart sang. There was something about seeing the dust fly in her rear view mirror that made her come alive. She turned up the volume on her radio, shut off the A/C and rolled down the windows. Her long hair flew around the car and out the window. Her elbow leaned on the window frame and her fingers tapped the steering wheel. She belted out the song on the

JILL BREUGEM

radio with the carefree abandon she had been missing in her life lately. As the song implied, it was her church.

Lucy and Tuck greeted her when she stepped out of her car. They wiggled and cried around her legs. "Hello, hello!" She petted them, leaning down to kiss each of them on their heads. "Okay, let me get my things, I love you, too."

"Hi honey!" her mother called from the front porch.

"Hi Mom!"

"I just put on a pot of tea, would you like a cup?"

"Love one!"

"How was your drive?" she called to Sadie as she entered the house.

"It was perfect. Where's Dad?"

"He's out back, building something around the garden, critters have been getting in there and stealing bulbs, and making a mess. Come, let's go sit on the front porch." Her mom carried a tray with tea cups and biscuits. Setting the tray down on a table, she went to her daughter and enveloped her in a big hug.

92

READ BETWEEN THE LINES

Sometimes you just need to come home, she thought to herself. She knew this was a good idea. Time to get away from the city, get out of that apartment, and get her mind off of Levi. She instantly felt like she could breathe better. She was able to get perspective here, and reminded herself that Levi was her agent and her friend. It was meant to be that way.

They settled into the big, white, wicker chairs with oversized red pillows and her mom went on to tell her about the latest news. It was a lovely distraction to hear the local gossip and various updates about family and friends. Her dad joined them as well and before long it was dinner time. Sadie enjoyed her mother's cooking, and helped her parents clean up the dinner dishes.

"How's Ally doing?" her mother asked.

"She's good, dating a guy named Gage. Things seem to be getting pretty serious."

"How about you honey, anyone special?"

"No, not right now. I do have a date Thursday with a guy I met at a party of a mutual friend."

"Oh that's nice. What's his name?"

"Yes, I'm looking forward to it. His name is Mick." she said, although Sadie didn't sound very

93

enthused. Her mother whom she was very close with, noticed.

"Hmmm, are you sure?" Her mom giggled and nudged her. "How is Levi these days, haven't seen him since Christmas."

"He's fine." she stated bluntly. "And I AM looking forward to going out with Mick," she said firmly.

"Okay," her mom said, raising both hands in defeat and knowing not to broach the subject any further. She knew the buttons not to push with Sadie.

Sadie dried the last dish and excused herself to put her bags in her room. While in there she checked her phone that she had deliberately turned off when she arrived. She didn't want the distraction.

On her phone was a funny Snapchat photo from Sam that made her smile and a text from Ally telling her that something was up with Gage. She responded to Ally, asking for more details, and told her she was probably reading into it too much. She went to Snapchat and sent Sam an equally silly picture.

Sadie laid down on the bed. Even though it was an old lumpy mattress, she knew a good sleep lay ahead of her. Fresh country air wafted in her open

READ BETWEEN THE LINES

bedroom window; a mix of fresh cut grass and her mother's beloved lavender. The only sound was the crush of gravel as the odd car went past the house. If she listened really hard she could hear the coyotes in the distance, their cries travelling miles over the night air. It was moments like this she wondered why she lived where she did.

She went down to spend the rest of her evening with her parents around the fire pit. Sharing old stories they stayed there until almost midnight.

In the morning Sadie felt refreshed from a great evening and a good sleep. She enjoyed a big breakfast and then got on the road. She had some things to do before her big date with Mick. She wanted to make sure she looked extra special. She was going to be ready for this date and give it a good shot; it was time to put her feelings for Levi to bed.

Chapter 12

First date

Sadie rolled out her mat and laid down in shavasana pose to wait for the yoga instructor. Staring at the ceiling in the nineteenth century building with its spacious and impressive detail, she felt much smaller than in her thoughts before. This was a beautiful space to clear the mind and centre herself. With only the whoosh sounds of mats dropping around her, she focused on her own breath that was currently catching and labored.

Coming into padmasana, also known as Lotus pose, Sadie closed her eyes and promised herself she would make sure to come to yoga more. She had created the kind of career that allowed her to make her own schedule, but somewhere along the line her well-being had fallen off the list. If she was going to keep up with the long, late nights to finish the two books, she was going to have to make herself more of a priority.

The class went by quickly and Sadie felt better than she had in weeks. She headed home to get ready for her date with Mick. She soaked in a hot bath, enjoyed a glass of wine, and sang along to Otis Redding coming from the speakers that she had installed in the master bathroom. Before dressing she applied lavender and grapefruit body oil that her friend Ally had made. Hopefully he liked the scent as much as she needed it to calm her down. She was both nervous and excited as she chose a simple black maxi dress to wear with a silver and turquoise statement necklace. She blew her hair dry and straightened it with her hot iron. Lastly she applied a small amount of makeup and went to get herself another glass of wine and wait.

She hadn't been on a date in months, not for lack of invitations, she just hadn't been interested. Spending time with Levi, her friends, and family, was all she wanted to do. Even now, had it not been for Ally's push and the events of the last couple days, she would have turned Mick down too.

READ BETWEEN THE LINES

Frantic thoughts started to pop up in her mind. She pictured the wedding. She pictured Barbara not letting her come to the wedding, and Levi going along with it, because it was his fiancées wishes after all. She pictured herself home alone drinking too much wine and sobbing on the kitchen floor. Eating ice cream out of the container, watching 'PS I Love You' on repeat. She pictured him ending their business relationship too, saying it was just too much for Barbara. She was making this all up in her head and it was driving her crazy!

At 7:30 sharp her phone rang for Mick to let her know he was there. She climbed into his Audi TT and buckled her seatbelt. He waited before pulling away, turning towards her to say hi. His smile was warm, his teeth perfect and white. He was dressed in jeans, an untucked navy button-down with a white V-neck shirt underneath, and laid back charcoal Vans. He smelled amazing; his cologne was very subtle, not poured on like some other dates she had been on. Sadie wasn't sure of the brand, but could smell hints of mint, cedarwood, and vanilla; it was quite a mix, but it worked well together.

She looked at him as they talked; taking note that he was better looking than she remembered. His hair was slicked back when they met, and today it was relaxed with no product. As she had first

99

noticed, his brown eyes stood out the most. They were a deep brown and rimmed with those thick eyelashes that women would die for. To top it off he had a chiseled jaw, sprinkled with a dusting of stubble, a straight nose and full lips. He could be a model, maybe he was? No, his business card suggested he worked in the financial district.

He seemed to be happy with what he saw too, smiling at her as they chatted effortlessly. Before long there were at the restaurant and headed to their table. They laughed about the day they met, and he told her about running into Ally.

"Sorry if you weren't expecting me to call. I hope you didn't give Ally too hard of a time over that?"

"Oh, I haven't had the chance to deal with her yet," Sadie teased.

"I was happy to make the first move, I actually prefer it," he said matter of fact and gave her a flirty smile. The waitress came over and took their drink order. He ordered a beer, and Sadie an Italian red. "You like red wine, right? Hope you don't mind I ordered for you?"

"No, that's okay." She did mind actually, I prefer wines from Argentina, but anyway...she thought to herself. She almost said it, and if she knew him better she would have. If it were Levi she would've. Live a little, Sadie.

Thankfully the conversation flowed; he asked her about the weekend away, and she gave him most of the details. She went on and explained how she and Levi had met, how he was her agent and very good friend.

"I am going to have to go to the bookstore tomorrow," he said, "grab me some Sadie Fisher books."

"Oh, I don't know that it would be your taste, Mick," Sadie joked, knowing her demographic was women who enjoyed romance.

"I'm a pretty romantic guy, Sadie. I might just like it, a lot. Which one should I start with?" He was very interested in her career, and they chatted about it for some time.

Mick told her that he was a stockbroker, falling in his dad's footsteps. He grew up in Toronto, in the affluent neighbourhood of Rosedale. He now lived south of the financial district in a ridiculously small but expensive bachelor apartment.

The band caught her attention, they were playing an array of alternative hits from the eighties. The band was good, the company was good, but soon Sadie found herself tired and feeling the wine.

"Mick, I've had a really great time, but, unfortunately a job hazard of mine, I tend to write all night, and am feeling the effects of it today. Do you mind if we call it a night?"

His surprise subsided to a warm smile and he said, "Of course. Promise me we can do this again sometime?"

"I would love to."

Chapter 13

Distractions

When Sadie rolled over the next morning and grabbed her phone she saw that she had two missed calls, one from Samantha, and one text message and call from Levi. She also had texts from Ally asking her about the night before and wanting every last juicy detail. She put her phone on silent when she went to bed last night, hoping to sleep in a bit this morning. The life of a writer was far from glamorous at times, but at least she was able to schedule her own hours, and she was grateful for that.

She had to admit her stomach flipped when she saw that Levi had messaged and called. She expected the others, but since Levi hadn't talked to her in a few days since the cottage, she was definitely relieved to see his name. She sent him a text right away to let him know that she saw he called.

"Hi, sorry to miss your call, I slept in today."

Her date with Mick couldn't have gone any better. He was gorgeous, successful, and very interesting. They had hours of great conversation and listened to a great band. She would be crazy not to want to go out with him again. So why was she so sad and confused about it then? And why was she so happy to hear from Levi?

She had been so tired and half way through the evening asked Mick to take her home. But once in the door, she headed to her computer and she wrote. She wrote for hours. She wrote about Levi. She finished the book. Yes, she wrote this book far faster than her others. Her editor would probably have a field day if they ever got their hands on it. But, it was the first book that she felt came directly from her heart and once she started, it just poured out.

The time on her phone said 11:30. She hadn't slept in this late in a while, but after all, she had

READ BETWEEN THE LINES

been up until early this morning. She didn't know why she did this to herself; she was definitely going to pay for this later.

Just then Levi responded. "Was starting to worry about you."

He was? What was he worried about?

"No need to worry, I stayed up until 4:00 writing, and then slept in."

"Whoa, you'll be tired today. Are you free for dinner?"

"Yep."

"Good, I will pick you up. Does 6:00 work?"

"Can we make it 7:00? I'm going out with Sam this afternoon."

"You bet, see you then."

She shot off a quick text to Ally and Sam and put on her gym clothes. She needed a quick run. She needed to clear her head and bring back the perspective she had when at her parents' house. She put on her watch, grabbed her iPod and earbuds, set it to her running mix, and headed out.

She wanted to hit up a local market and planned to meet up with her friend Samantha for lunch around 1:00, so she didn't have long for a run.

Samantha lived just north of the city in a house she bought after her first movie. Samantha had been acting for years, in Canadian shows, but hit it big when she starred in a Hollywood movie filmed in Toronto. They cast the lead male role with a Hollywood heartthrob and then cast the rest of the movie in Hollywood North, as Toronto was called, along with Vancouver, due to the high volume of production that took place north of the border.

Samantha herself had shied away from dating after a much publicized relationship with an actor ended badly. She had found the whole experience invasive, embarrassing and painful. It was a very sad time for her, but she was thankful she had friends like Sadie and Ally nearby, which wouldn't have been the case if she had moved to LA like others in her industry frequently did.

Sadie jogged west across Yonge to tour some of the older neighbourhoods. She didn't get very far when the sharp pain in her foot reminded her that she cut it only a few days ago. She ran anyway, for thirty minutes. When she made it back to her building she was limping like a fool.

"Ms. Fisher, are you okay?" Jones, the concierge, ran to her aid. She was so thankful for Jones, he was like a father away from home.

READ BETWEEN THE LINES

"I hurt my foot the other day, stupid to have thought I could go out for a run." She let him help her to the elevator and then told him she was fine to carry on from there. Once she got to her apartment she headed straight for the shower. She grimaced while she took her blood soaked sock off. After her shower she bandaged her foot up good and settled on ballerina flats instead of her usual sandals in order to hide the bandages.

Her visit with Samantha was exactly what she needed. They met in the area of Yorkville at an Italian restaurant. They enjoyed lots of carbs, dessert and some expensive wine. She told Samantha everything, starting with her feelings for Levi, and then what happened at the cottage, and her date with Mick. She admitted she was confused about everything and the stress of the books was getting to her.

Samantha admitted she wasn't surprised about Levi, and figured it was only a matter of time. They had a good laugh about the cottage, seeing the comic relief in what happened now after the fact. Samantha told her to give Mick a chance just like Ally had, since Levi was in a committed relationship. Sadie figured Ally must have filled her in already on her own opinion.

"Hey, if you need to get away from it all, you are welcome to come with me." Samantha told Sadie about some upcoming roles and future trips to Hollywood. Sadie promised to consider the proposal. She knew many would have jumped at a proposal like that, but she had at least one book she needed to finish and not a lot of time to do it in.

Chapter 14

Dinner

Sadie met Levi at the front of her building so that he didn't have to park. She was half expecting to see Barbara and was relieved when she saw that it was just him. She was really nervous about how it was going to go today, if everything was going to be weird, but Levi soon put her at ease after she climbed into the car.

"Hey Sunshine, looking good friend." She was wearing a red sundress that he had commented on before. She wore her hair down but instead of blow drying it, she had left it to dry naturally and it fell in beachy waves around her shoulders.

"Hi!" If there was someone who was looking good, it was definitely Levi. He had a fresh haircut, he was clean shaven, and the seductive scent of the sandalwood and orange was hanging subtly around him. She wanted to dive on him with a huge hug but she held back.

"I'm going to head to Plum, is that okay?"

"Sounds great to me," Sadie answered.

"How was your day?"

"It was good, slept in - as you know, and went for a run. I had a good visit with Sam."

"You ran with your foot?" Levi interjected.

"Yeah, not my brightest idea. I needed to get out. How about you? How was your day?"

"Just some meetings, nothing special."

Small talk continued until they were at the restaurant and settled at a table.

"So, how was your date last night?" He waited no time to ask, and without a hint of jealousy. I guess he was taking a higher road than he had at Piper's barbeque.

"Good, the band was cool. They were very retro, old school, kind of reminded me of The Smiths. They sang my favourite, 'I Know It's

Over', I loved it." Sadie paused and then added, "My dinner was delicious. I would definitely go back there again." Was she rambling? Did he need all that detail at once? Why didn't she talk slower and elaborate, and make it clear that it was amazing.

"So, how was Hunky Mick? What's his story?" he asked, ignoring the other details about her date that she shared.

"Very nice guy. He's a couple years younger, very successful. He's a stockbroker." She tried to catch his expression through her eyelashes as she looked down.

"Are you seeing him again?" His questions were curt and blunt. Maybe he was jealous?

"Yes, I think so." Sadie started playing with her food, not wanting to make eye contact. When she finally looked up Levi was looking right at her, no expression on his face. He had a lot of nerve. Why shouldn't she see him again? It's not like Levi was available. He was very clear at the cottage how he felt about Barbara, and she needed someone in her life, too.

"What?" she asked, feeling perturbed by his attitude.

"Nothing," he paused. "So how's the book coming? On schedule for September? Editor will have it for a couple months and hopefully we can hit the holiday time frame. That's the goal anyway." His tone changed to all business, something he never did with Sadie.

"Yes, sure thing," Sadie said shifting in her seat.

"Ideally we would've wanted to get it to them sooner, but I'll put a rush on the editing."

"Okay."

"Did you call John about the cover?"

"No, but I'll do that soon, I want to make sure the story is where I want it, and that I'm confident about the title."

"Good, ok, should keep on as planned. Hate to miss the holiday sales." He continued with a certain animosity, and she didn't like it one bit. He was acting like a scolding parent, a micromanager. He clearly had a chip on his shoulder about something.

"We won't miss any holiday sales," Sadie said then asked, "Levi, what's your problem?"

"Nothing, there's no problem." He answered, again with no expression on his face. His warm welcome when she first got in the car was long gone. He was being cold now, and she didn't like it one bit. Where was this coming from? Was it the

READ BETWEEN THE LINES

cottage? Mick? Was it because she wasn't sharing much about the book?

"I think there is, you're acting weird. You almost sound like you're scolding me. You've known my timing all along."

"What happened at the cottage? Why did you run to the lake?" Fantastic, first a scolding about the book, and now he was going to ask about this?

"I told you, I felt nauseous. I had too much wine."

"I don't believe you."

"You don't believe me? You saw the wine bottle! You cleaned up the glass!"

"Sadie." He said her name firmly and continued to look straight into her eyes. "Tell me why you felt the need to run out of the cottage and down to the lake."

She looked down at her hands, refusing to look him in the eye. She wasn't prepared to have this conversation. She didn't know when she would be.

"Do you really want to know?" she asked.

"Yes, I want to know."

"Levi. What does it matter?" She was stalling. She wouldn't look at him. She grabbed her wine and

113

drank it all in one gulp. He poured her more. Great, here we go a repeat of the cottage. She would be slurring in no time. What was she going to say? What was he expecting?

"I want to know," he whispered. Sadie looked up. His face had relaxed, and his eyes were softer. She wanted to tell him. But what if he didn't feel the same? What if he was just asking so that he could tell her that he was happy with Barbara and that she needed to move on? That their friendship couldn't continue the way it was like this, that they needed more boundaries and that it wasn't fair to Barbara, especially now knowing how Sadie felt? Or worse what Barbara had suspected was true, and they would need to cut ties? And that he might not be able to continue the business relationship either. He was the best in the business and she needed him.

Sadie wanted to bolt again. She was NOT ready for this conversation, but maybe she should just move on before he didn't even give her a choice and moved on without her.

Just then his phone rang, he looked at the screen and excused himself.

She wondered who it could be. He didn't normally excuse himself to take a call around her, and considering the conversation they were having she found it very strange. If it was Barbara she

READ BETWEEN THE LINES

would lose it! How dare he quiz her like this and take a call from Barbara, leaving her at the table alone.

"I have to go, Sadie." His face was white as a ghost. He grabbed his keys from the table and looked around for the waiter.

"Is everything okay?" She was worried. He didn't look good. He looked like someone had died.

"Yes, I need to go," he said.

"Okay," she answered, but he had already gone over to the bar and paid the waiter. Sadie's face heated and she fought back tears. She wasn't going to let him see her upset, no way. He came back to the table and hesitated. He opened his mouth and closed it again.

"Go Levi." She waved her hand. "I can catch a cab, or Uber…" she said nonchalantly.

"You sure?" He was asking her if she was sure. He should be offering to take her home first. But no, it appeared as though he was leaving her there. Was it Barbara? Was she angry at him and giving him an ultimatum? Was the call a perfect excuse to end this conversation? He normally told her everything. To just leave with no explanation was completely out of character.

115

"Of course, don't be silly, go." She forced a smile, and waved her hand again. He thanked her and was gone.

Sadie felt the hot tear slide down her cheek. She was stunned. She was heartbroken. I guess that's it, she thought. She stayed frozen at the table for what seemed like hours, and finished her wine.

Her phone vibrated on the table. Thinking it was Levi calling to come back and get her, she answered it without even looking.

"Hi," she answered.

"Hey, I know I'm breaking all of the rules of dating and playing it cool, but I had a great time last night and was thinking of you." It was Mick. Hunky Mick. Take that Levi.

"I had a great time, too," Sadie answered with a small smile. Considering what had just happened with Levi, she was delighted to hear from Mick. "Do you want to grab a drink or a coffee or something? I'm free right now." Why not break all the dating rules she thought.

"Sadie, I would love to! I can be there in ten minutes."

"I'm over at Plum, I came here for dinner with Levi, but he had to go for a…an emergency." she improvised. "So, it'll take me twenty minutes to get

READ BETWEEN THE LINES

back to my apartment. Unless there's somewhere we can meet?"

"Stay where you are, I'll be there in a few, I'm close by."

Sadie hung up the phone and went in the washroom to check her appearance and touch up her lipstick. "This will have to do," she said aloud, running her fingers under her eyes to remove some mascara that fell with her tears. She headed out front to wait for her handsome ride.

Chapter 15

Rescue

"Well, Levi is crazy to leave you at a restaurant on your own, but am I ever glad he did." Mick flirted.

"He had an emergency or something," Sadie mumbled as she got into his car and put on her seatbelt. She looked over at Mick and gave him a smile. "Thank you so much, I owe you one."

"You owe me nothing. It's my pleasure," he said.

He looked so good, she was crazy to have debated seeing him again. Any woman would be thrilled to be sitting where she was. He was the definition of a beautiful man. Tonight he was wearing a black V-neck t-shirt that showed his tanned and toned arms and worn jeans with dark suede loafers.

He chuckled to himself and said, "I am more than happy to come pick you up anytime, Sadie."

"Thanks."

"Hey, are you okay?"

"Oh yeah, I'm fine. It's fine. "

"You sound like you're trying to convince yourself. Was it something with Levi?"

"I don't have a clue what's up with him. But I'm okay, no worries." She considered telling him the truth. Explaining that she was really upset, confused, and didn't know what was going on, but ultimately, she didn't want to talk to him about Levi. If she started she might not be able to stop herself, and then Mick definitely wouldn't want to see her again.

"Where do you want to grab a drink?"

"How about the Lounge over on Wellington, they usually have a good band on Friday nights."

"Sounds good."

"So what's a good looking guy like you doing with no plans on a Friday night?"

READ BETWEEN THE LINES

"Well, when I called you, I was hoping I would get some plans." He winked.

It's already after 8:00 she thought to herself. Strange time to be calling. Not enough notice for a date, too early for a booty call, and they certainly weren't at that stage yet.

When they got to the venue, Mick watched her walking ahead of him, admiring what he saw. Levi was crazy leaving her alone, he thought to himself. This girl was gorgeous. Surely men fell at her feet everywhere she went. She was taller than most women, curvy but lean, and her hair was long and golden. She had the kind of face that made you look twice, then it made you want to stare and dissect each perfect feature. He was surprised she wasn't an actress or a model instead of an author. Not that she wasn't a good writer; when he told his sister that he was going on a date with Sadie Fisher, she freaked out. She requested signed copies of books, pictures, and an introduction.

He knew Sadie would happily do all that for his sister and more. In the short time he'd known her he could tell she was a really nice person. But he wasn't about to ask her after only a couple dates, he had to play it a cool for a while. He didn't mind swooping in to pick her up tonight, after all he was hoping she would be free when he called.

121

The nightclub was dark, and her eyes were still adjusting when Mick grabbed her from behind by the hips and moved her towards their seats. She found the move unsettling. This was their second date, and it wasn't that Sadie was being a prude. She was getting the impression in this short time that Mick was a bit of a ladies man, and she wasn't going to be just another notch in his belt.

She removed his hands while looking up over her shoulder at him. "Sorry," he said over the loud music, smiling sweetly and holding his hands up.

She smiled back and said something quickly as to not draw any more awkwardness to the moment. "Have you been here before, Mick?"

"No, first time. I'm going to go get us drinks. Be right back." He returned with their drinks and pulled up a chair beside her to get a good view of the band. The singer was a beautiful woman with an Amy Winehouse beehive and a pointy bustier. She was singing an oldie by the Supremes, and there were a number of people on the dance floor already. It was still early to be dancing by nightclub standards, but it was easy to see why they were. The band was THAT good.

Mick leaned in close to talk to her. "They're fantastic."

READ BETWEEN THE LINES

"Yes, they are," she answered. "Do you dance?" She motioned to the floor.

"Unfortunately it would take several of these to get me up there," he said, as he nodded his drink towards her. "And since I'm driving tonight, that's not possible."

"What is it with you guys needing liquid courage to dance?"

"Well, I can only speak for myself and say I have no rhythm and it would be quite the spectacle," he paused, "And I want to see you again." He smiled at her, nudging her side with his.

Her face broke into a smile as she nudged him back. He was really nice to look at and he smelled really good. She should really try to focus on him, but her thoughts kept going back to Levi. Mick ordered them another drink. They chatted for a while about where they grew up, went to school, and careers. The conversation flowed. But she knew she was a little off and she knew that he knew it too.

"I know I asked you before, but are you okay? You seem to have lots on your mind."

"I'm okay, sorry, yes, lots on my mind..." and then she added, "You must think I'm a real dud.

123

Last night I needed to go home early, tonight I might need to do the same."

"Hey, don't worry about it. I'm ready whenever you are. Lots of time to get to know each other."

His patience with her in that moment spoke volumes to her. He must be thinking what is wrong with this chick? She was all over the place and after he came to pick her up tonight, he deserved more than she was emotionally giving.

Sadie stood up, straightened her dress and put out her hand.

"What are you doing Sadie?"

"It's a slow song, I'm asking you to dance."

"Sadie, I told you I can't dance."

"Surely you know how to slow dance," she replied.

Smiling, but reluctantly, he stood up, took her hand, and let her lead him to the dance floor. He took one hand and held it in his, and put the other around her waist, while she rested her other hand up around his neck.

"This is nice."

Smiling, she nodded, "Yes, it's not that bad, dancing with me?"

READ BETWEEN THE LINES

"No, Sadie, it's not bad at all." He kissed her on the cheek.

"I hope that wasn't too forward," he said.

Smiling she shook her head no, and squeezed his hand.

He liked this girl, a lot. He was in trouble.

Chapter 16

Cover for Me

Sadie met with John the next day about her book cover. She asked him to create two covers. Thankfully he didn't ask why when she asked him not to share the details with anyone - especially Levi. It surprised her that she was still writing about Levi considering how she was feeling about him these days, but the story continued to write itself.

"Sadie, just to confirm, I'm making two covers for two different books?"

"Yes, that's right." She sat across from John at a coffee shop, his iPad in front of him, taking notes. He was very creative and eccentric. He always had the best ideas and the best taste. Sadie had been working with John since her first cover. He was sought after in the industry and she was fortunate that he was never too busy to take on her jobs.

"Okay...you have never published two books at once before."

"I know, and I might not. I just want to be ready."

"And you don't want me to talk about it with Levi or Piper or anyone?" he questioned.

"That's right." He raised one eyebrow at her, but being the professional that he was, he let it go and got to work.

"Okay...let's review what you want on the first cover. The photographer and the model - what's the name?"

"It's called 'Pictures of You'."

"What was your first thought for the cover?"

"I was thinking simple, a camera, maybe the screen. Or a picture of their travels."

"Well, from the snippet you sent me, I was thinking the same, a camera too, maybe the Eiffel Tower in the background, maybe even make a picture, like a polaroid shot?"

READ BETWEEN THE LINES

"Oh, I love it, John." She knew where he was going with this, and knew she wouldn't be disappointed.

"Okay, I'll draw up a few mock-ups, and send them over within a few weeks."

"Fantastic!" She took a deep breath.

"Okay the second book - you didn't send me a title. Do you have one yet?"

"No, I've been torn between a few. But I know what I want on the cover."

"What were you thinking?"

"The lake."

"Just a lake?"

"Yes. The lake, a canoe."

"The snippet you sent over had a scene where the couple were in the canoe. Any particular lake you are envisioning? I could research, sketch a scene of the lake, the scenery, a canoe with two people - just their outlines."

"Sounds great and yes, I was envisioning Lake Rousseau." She could feel her face heating up, giving her away. She took a drink of her tea and looked away.

129

"Levi's lake?" he asked. The writing world was a small community and John had been up to Levi's cottage many times.

"Well, it's not just Levi's lake," she replied getting her back up. "There are hundreds of cottages on Lake Rousseau." She made a guffaw sound with her mouth agape and shifted in her seat.

"Ah, yes, there are." He grinned from ear to ear at her. He had been friends with Levi for years, and was not a stranger to Levi's cottage.

"What?"

"Nothing." Still grinning.

"Stop it, John." Sadie said trying to be firm.

"Stop what?"

"You know what." She looked out the shop window, refusing to make eye contact with him. "It's a beautiful lake, John."

"Yes, I can see why it would inspire you." Still grinning.

"Remember that you promised me, you won't talk about the covers with anyone," she said, looking him firmly in the eye.

"Nope, no one, not even Max." Max was his newborn baby. And he was still grinning.

READ BETWEEN THE LINES

"Funny," she said while rolling her eyes and giving him a wink. "How are Sarah and Max doing these days? Any new pictures? You must have hundreds on that phone." Sadie was eagerly trying to change the subject.

They looked at baby pictures and went their separate ways. That was enough to deter him from where he was headed. He had figured it out in one short conversation. What would happen if Levi read a couple chapters? What if he read the book? She trusted John, she knew he wouldn't say anything to anyone.

Sadie couldn't wait to see what he came back to her with over the next month. It was at this point she felt her books came to life. The cover was probably the most important selling feature to any book. It was the cover that captured the reader's attention and the synopsis that urged them to make a commitment to her story. Without a good cover the words don't stand a chance.

Chapter 17

Mick

Mick and Sadie spent the next couple months getting to know each other better, going for walks, the movies, and cooking for each other. They were taking it slow. He was easy to be around, he was charming, and fun. They always had a great time, but even still, she found her thoughts were always on Levi.

Levi had checked in with her the day after leaving her at the restaurant, but she had been with Mick at the time, so he didn't say much. He made a quick apology but never gave an explanation. Did he owe her one? Their friendship was feeling the strain of whatever was going on. His texts and phone calls were now specifically work related. No more lunch visits or hanging out on a patio on a Sunday afternoon. The close friendship they once shared seemed to be gone, for now.

She wasn't entirely sure if the relationship changed because he was giving her space to enjoy her new relationship with Mick, if he was taking the space to satisfy Barbara, or if this was just the way things were going to be. Either way, it made her a little angry and very sad. She missed him. She missed him a lot.

After a delicious meal that Mick had made them at his apartment, they fell onto the couch together. Their cheeks were rosy from the after dinner aperitif, a dry sherry that they sipped on while cozied up on the couch. He grabbed the remote and started to mindlessly click through shows, stopping on a movie.

"Come here, you're too far away," Mick said, grabbing her side and pulling her towards him. His hand moved up and down her outer thigh. She had a feeling that this might go somewhere tonight. They had been dating for some time. They were clearly attracted to each other, but every time Mick had tried to make a move, Sadie had an excuse. She simply was not in a rush to move things along.

READ BETWEEN THE LINES

She cuddled into his side, letting one hand rest on his chest. "I'm so full Mick, I feel like a beached whale right now." He kissed the top of her head as if to put her at ease.

"Can I get you a drink?"

"No, thank you, I have to drive home in a little while."

"You can stay the night Sadie," But as fast as his words left his mouth, she had pulled away. It wasn't going to happen tonight, again. He had been very patient recently, but it was starting to wear thin.

"Sadie, are you attracted to me?"

"Yes, of course!" she exclaimed.

"You know you're the only person I'm dating," he assured her.

"Same," Sadie answered.

"I think we've spent a lot of time together in the last couple months, don't you? We've gotten to know each other pretty well," he stated.

"Yes," she pulled away and looked up into his eyes, then looking down at her hands.

"I really like you," he said and then added, "a lot."

"I like you too," she responded.

"You like me?" he repeated.

"Yes, of course I do." Sadie said, her tone changing now as well. She crossed her arms close to her body.

"Sadie, I don't mean to make you upset, or pressure you. I'm just interested in taking it to the next step, and I want to know that you are too."

Sadie's phone buzzed, and ironically it was Levi.

"Just a second Mick, I need to take this." She was so thankful for Levi in that moment. It was a huge sign from the universe. She leaned forward to pick up her phone and answer it. Behind her Mick's expression was none too pleased.

"You want to take it?" His tone was angry. "I think we need to finish this conversation."

She answered the phone anyway. "Hi Levi, what's up?"

"Can you talk? Is it a good time?" he asked.

Looking at the look on Mick's face she knew the real answer was no, but assured him it was fine.

"Of course. What's going on? You sound upset."

READ BETWEEN THE LINES

"Hi. It's my dad, he's not doing well. Are you around? I need to talk to you."

"Yes of course, are you home? I can head over?"

"I'd like that," pausing Levi said, "I have missed you, Sadie." His voice cracked. He sounded like he had been crying and the thought broke her heart.

A lump formed in her throat and she squeaked out a goodbye. "Me too, I'll see you soon."

She stood up and turned back to Mick, "I'm sorry, I have to go."

"Everything okay?"

She sat back down beside him wringing her hands. "I don't know. Its Levi's dad, he isn't well. I need to go see him."

Mick looked at her like he wanted to say something. His face lacked the concern and emotion he normally would have for her. Instead he looked angry. She got up and walked over to grab her cardigan and bag. As she dug in her bag for her keys, Mick came over to her and put his arms around her. He was trying to calm his emotions. She went rigid, and he let go.

"Mick, thanks for dinner, I'm sorry."

"Where's Barbara?" he asked. He couldn't help himself.

"What?"

"Where's Barbara? You know, his girlfriend."

"I don't know, why are you asking?" Sadie's back was up, and she was not happy where the conversation was going.

"Just wondering why he's asking you to come and not his girlfriend?"

"Mick, I'm not sure you realize, but Levi is not just my agent, he has been a really good friend of mine for years." She said sternly. How dare he be questioning her about going to see Levi? They were very close friends, his dad was sick and he needed her. Why was he being so crusty?

"Yes, but why wouldn't his girlfriend be there with him, why does mine have to go?"

"Seriously Mick?" Her head was cocked to the side and her hand was on her hip. She continued, "Why you are asking me about his girlfriend? You know I'm his friend, and when a friend is going through something, you go see them." She walked away from him and towards the door. She wasn't sure if it was because it was Levi, or the fact that Mick was sounding insecure and jealous, traits she wasn't very fond of, but she could see the end in

READ BETWEEN THE LINES

sight for this relationship. Part of her felt a pang of guilt.

"Sadie, if you're such good friends, why did he leave you at that restaurant that night?" His voice started to raise. "Why have the two of you barely talked in weeks?"

"I don't know what that was all about, I'm sure I'll find out," she paused, "And anyway, I'm a grown woman Mick, I told him to go on ahead without me that night." Dropping her bag at her feet and kneeling while she put on her shoes. She was so angry. "Don't sit here and pass judgements on Levi from one night. You don't even know him."

"Oh I know how he feels about you, Sadie." he mumbled.

"What's that supposed to mean?" She stood up and looked him squarely in the eye.

"He wants more than just friendship with you, Sadie. That's been obvious since I first met you."

"Mick…" Sadie tried to stop the discussion, with a shake of her head. She needed to go see Levi. She didn't want to talk about this right now. She reached for the doorknob. He put his arm on the door to hold it shut, forcing her to look at him.

"And so do you, Sadie."

139

"Mick, I'm not doing this with you right now, I have to go." He moved his arm, tilted his head towards her and leaned in for a kiss. Sadie turned her face and it landed on her cheek. She looked up into the hurt in his eye. She was angry at him, even though she knew what he said was true, at least when it came to how she felt.

"Good bye, Mick."

Mick watched her go and knew it was the last time he would see her.

Chapter 18

Explanations

Her heart beat fast and her hands shook as she knocked on Levi's door. He opened the door, took her hand, and pulled her in.

"I'm sorry, Sadie," he said and pulled her into a hug. "I should have explained. I shouldn't have just left you at the restaurant, without saying something." Dark circles outlined his eyes, his shoulders were slumped, and he looked sad and tired. Sadie had never seen him like this before and it killed her. He led her into the living room and they sat down on his couch.

Turning towards him she said, "Levi, you don't have to tell me anything. What you do, it's none of my business," knowing full well that she wanted him to tell her everything. Every last detail.

"Sadie, of course I tell you these things. I should have explained, and I shouldn't have left you. And I shouldn't have waited two months to explain."

"It's okay, I'm sure you had a good reason, Levi," she assured him.

"Even still, no excuse. I can't believe I just left you there." He looked down, then back up into her eyes. "He came to get you, didn't he?"

"Mick did, yes."

"I figured when I called you, and the two of you were together."

"What's going on with your dad?" Sadie asked with concern, ignoring his statements about Mick.

"He's not well." He choked. His elbows were on his knees and his face in his hands. A lone tear landed on his thigh and glistened on his tanned skin. She leaned towards him and rested her hand where the tear fell.

"I'm here now." She patted his leg. Levi placed his hand over hers and gently squeezed.

READ BETWEEN THE LINES

"What's happened with your dad, Levi?"

Levi's dad had stage 4 dementia, but still lived at home with Levi's mom and had a nurse that visited. Sadie had told Levi her experience with dementia and had suggested to him that maybe he should consider putting his dad in a nursing home. It was the only time that he seemed significantly angry with her. She felt terrible after and decided she wouldn't broach the subject again.

Sadie had her own experience with dementia with a neighbour on her floor at the condo. Mrs. Palmer had on more than one occasion, mistaken Sadie for her daughter. She would find her wandering the halls, forgetting what she had left her apartment for, and even trying to enter ones that weren't hers. Sometimes Mrs. Palmer would smile sweetly and other times she would be distraught and incoherent. There were times Mrs. Palmer was even aggressive. Sadie had Mrs. Palmer's daughter on speed dial. Eventually, they had to put her into a home.

Levi's dad's dementia was even more advanced and the stories he shared were heartbreaking. Although his dad had memories of years gone by, he couldn't remember if he had breakfast or why he wasn't allowed to drive his car. Sometimes he would leave the house and disappear, creating panic for the family. Other times he would be found in his favourite place, his workshop. He would be working with tools like he had done for forty years, and suddenly be standing there holding a running power tool, not sure what to do with it. Levi was concerned for his safety and his mom's safety, but she was adamant that her husband stay at home with her.

His father fell down the stairs the night they were at the restaurant. He had been in the hospital ever since with a broken hip and his health was declining rapidly. Levi was told that his dad wouldn't be coming home this time. He was spending night and day there and it was clearly taking a toll on him.

Sadie realized it had been two months since that night in the restaurant. All this time had passed and she hadn't been there for him. She had been busy with Mick, thinking Levi didn't need her. As much as she hated the notion, she hoped Barbara had been there for him. Everyone needed somebody during difficult times like this. She couldn't bear the thought of him dealing with it alone.

"How can I help, Levi?" She asked.

"No, nothing, I just needed to talk to you. I missed you so much." He looked her square in the eye. She felt her face blush. She had missed him too.

READ BETWEEN THE LINES

"I missed you too."

"I also wanted to finally explain why I left you that night in the restaurant."

"Don't give it another thought. I'd like to bring some meals by for you and your mom. You must be getting tired of the food there."

"We wouldn't say no to that," he said with a small smile. "We're pretty tired of the food in the hospital and the surrounding areas."

"Consider it done. How about now, have you eaten? Can I whip something up? Run out and grab you something?"

"No, no. I'm good. I just needed to see you, explain. Do you forgive me?"

"Of course, nothing to forgive." She looked down at her hand, still on his thigh. "I have to admit, I thought it was out of character. But, I didn't think of something like this, I thought maybe it was Barbara."

"Never," he said and squeezed her hand again. "I'm going to go over and pick up my mom. Thanks for coming over and for hearing me out."

"Of course." They stood up at the same time. He held her hands as they faced each other. A small smile crept on his face as he squeezed her hands. No

145

sooner was a smile also across hers as she wrapped her arms around his neck and gave him a long hug. They had been best friends for the last seven years, she wasn't going to let that go again. Even if she couldn't be with Levi in the way she so badly desired, she didn't want to lose his friendship or feel the way she had these last couple months, ever again.

"I'll call you tomorrow before I bring over food, probably around 11:30. Does that work?"

"Sounds great. My mom will be happy to see you."

"I look forward to seeing her too. And your dad, although I know he might not remember me."

Walking her to the door, he kissed her cheek as she left. He wanted to ask her how Mick was. God he hated that guy, he just couldn't bring himself to ask. Maybe tomorrow.

READ BETWEEN THE LINES

Chapter 19

Read Between the Lines

He knew Sadie wasn't home yet, she had messaged that she was on her way to an appointment but would be back in just over an hour. He didn't normally let himself in when she wasn't there except when he was on plant duty when she was on one of her travels, but tonight he wanted to surprise her. Things had been strained between them. He knew he was mostly to blame and he wanted to make it up to her. She had been a godsend to him and his mom over the last week with visits and meals. She had been the sunshine they so badly needed.

He picked up a bouquet of flowers and take-out from her favourite Thai restaurant.

He tossed his keys on the counter, laid the flowers down momentarily, and put the food in the oven on low to stay warm. He found a vase above the fridge, popped the flowers in some water and placed them on the island. Getting her flowers would seem weird for most friends to do but they were different. He checked the fridge and sure enough there were several of his favourite beers. He opened up an Austrian beer and went over to the couch to sit down.

He would check some email and message Sadie in a bit to find out her timing. He had a few emails from one of his needy clients and their publicists. They wanted to set up more tour dates and didn't like Levi's opinion that they were done touring. She was a diva of an author, sales were slowing down to a crawl and the book had been out for longer than usual to warrant tour dates. The author needed to move on to another writing project. He would address it tomorrow, he wasn't in the mood for conflict today. Today was a good day.

As he was putting his feet up on the coffee table he nudged her laptop. "I wonder how her book is coming," he thought. Instinctively he tapped on the space bar and saw that not only was there no

READ BETWEEN THE LINES

password to enter, she was right in the middle of writing. She must have simply set it aside when she went out. She didn't have any sort of sleep mode set up for the screen.

He should close the lid, he thought to himself. That would be the right thing to do. That would be what Sadie would want. She hated when he looked at her work before it was finished. Maybe if he closed the lid it would put it into the sleep mode and ask for a password. As close as they were, he didn't know what the password could be. Close the lid. Certainly he had to respect her privacy.

He couldn't help himself. He placed the computer on his lap and went on to read at least a dozen pages. He read enough pages to get a really good sense of the storyline. What the hell?

What had he just read? Stunned, he placed the laptop back on the coffee table and sat back on the couch. He ran his hands through his hair and up and down his face like he was just waking up from a deep slumber. Wow. He wanted to keep reading but knew that Sadie would be here soon, and the last thing he wanted was for her to catch him in the act. She would be furious and potentially deny it all. He felt an incredible sense of guilt wave over him, and then the excitement of what he just read landed in his belly.

151

It wasn't the story that Sadie had pitched to Piper. It was not the story about the model and photographer that she had told them sitting in Piper's office. It was not the story she had confirmed in the car following the meeting with Piper. It was not the story that she had shared details with him several times since. Did that story even exist? Is that why she wouldn't look him in the eye in his car when he questioned her?

He had to admit, he liked this new story better. Much better. A slow smile appeared across his face and he had a feeling it would be there a while. In between the lines of this tale weaved a story that was all too familiar.

The story was 100% undeniably written about the two of them. It was about Sadie and him! It was their love story.

She messaged that she would be awhile yet. He wanted to get over to see his mom and dad at the hospital. He knew he better go. He would need to confront Sadie at some point, but what about Mick? She seemed happy with Mick. There were things he had to take care of, things he had to do, and he had to get out of here now. He couldn't see Sadie yet. Not yet.

He left her a note on the counter to check to see what was in the oven and turned it off.

READ BETWEEN THE LINES

He was giddy. He was elated. He was Tom-Cruise-jumping-on-a-couch-happy.

He locked up and took the stairs down just for something to do, and because he was simply too excited to wait for an elevator. The rush of running down the stairs, flying around the corners with each flight made him feel like a kid. He came out on the main floor through doors by the concierge desk, all sweaty and silly.

"Hey, Jones!" Levi greeted the doorman with a high-five and headed to the parking garage with a skip in his step. Jones looked after him with bewilderment and a chuckle.

"Hello, Mr. Townsend. Nice to see you," Jones said looking from Levi to the door to the stairs and back to Levi. "Did you just run down all sixty flights?"

"You bet, Jones. You bet I did!"

Confused, Jones leaned towards the elevators to see if they were working. "Well, enjoy the rest of your day," he called after him. Levi was already hopping into his car and making his way out of the parking garage, the happiest he had been in a long time.

Chapter 20

Thankful

Sadie unlocked her apartment door and smelled the yummy aroma of her favourite green curry vegetable Thai dish. She locked the door behind her and went to the kitchen where she found a note from Levi, along with a mixed bouquet of flowers. He had wrote 'Thank you for being you,' and told her to check the oven for her dinner and that he couldn't stay.

A huge smile broke on her face as she pulled the dishes out of the oven and got herself a fork and plate. "Yummy! You are the bomb, Levi!" She announced to the empty room. She poured herself a glass of sparkling water and hopped up onto a stool at the island to enjoy her delicious meal.

Levi had outdone himself with the flowers, a combination of hydrangeas, peonies and tulips. They were stunning. Not that he needed to do that or get dinner, but she knew it was his way of saying sorry, and saying thank you for being there. She knew things were getting back to normal for them. She thought about how strained things had been over the last few months, for the first time in their friendship. She was hoping to see him tonight but he said he wanted to get over to the hospital which she understood. She texted him instead.

"You spoiled me."

"The least I could do," he answered.

"Not necessary, but not complaining."

"They say the way to a girl's heart is food and flowers, don't they?"

"I think its food for guys and diamonds for girls, but I'm not just any girl," she joked.

"No you're not. Is it working by the way?" he texted.

"Is what working?" she asked, initially confused by his question.

"Nothing. Talk to you later."

READ BETWEEN THE LINES

"Ciao xo," she responded. Was he talking about *her* heart? Is that what he was implying? She smiled at her phone, sat a little straighter, and finished her delicious meal. Not before taking a few funny photos of her food and texting some friends. There was a running joke amongst the crowd to send pictures of food to each other.

Thinking it was strange to not hear from Ally yet, as they were always quick to respond to each other, she went to her laptop to write. She had some more inspiration. Deadlines were fast approaching, she needed to spend as much time as possible getting the book(s) done. Still unsure of which one would go to print, Sadie spent equal time on both. Grabbing her laptop from the coffee table, she headed to her office and put on some music.

In her email inbox were two book covers as promised by her designer, John. His work was stunning as usual. He knew her taste so well; book after book he nailed it. She immediately sent him approvals for both book covers.

The cover for her book about Levi was simply perfect. She could frame it and probably would one day. It was a simple and familiar view of the beautiful Lake Rousseau in the Muskoka. You could literally be looking out on the lake, standing on Levi's dock. The lake was surrounded with pine trees as well as the autumn colours of birch, maple, and oak, the rocky outcropping of the Canadian Shield at her feet. It had to be her favourite place to be in the world. She was hoping to go up soon and do some writing. The cover made her long to be there, she knew for many reasons.

The fall was a beautiful time at the lake. While many would close their cottages for the season around Canada's Thanksgiving in early October, Levi's was open year round. Levi and Sadie would get excited about the cooler temperatures and the calmness of the quiet lake in their canoe. They would bundle up in blankets around a roaring campfire or by the warm glow of the indoor/outdoor fireplace. They enjoyed hiking amongst the beautiful colours of autumn. They frequently cross country skied with friends on the same trails in the winter, loving the crisp temperatures, the sound of your own breath mixed with the crunch of snow.

Also in her inbox was a plan for a book tour starting mid-November for three weeks. It would get her home in plenty of time for Christmas shopping and parties. It was cutting it close, but she had brought this upon herself, hadn't she? It was a tour across a few major cities in Canada and the US, and a new stop this year in London, England. There was a plan for more in the new year.

READ BETWEEN THE LINES

Maybe she would see if Ally would want to get away for a bit and come with her on the tour. It could be tiring and straining on someone travelling and not sleeping well for three weeks, but it could also be a lot of fun. They could squeeze in some a great meals, sight-seeing, and shopping. Sadie quickly dropped Ally another line.

Her phone began to ring; it was Ally.

"Hey you, you'll never believe what I'm eating and the most beautiful flowers I'm looking at, and who they are from!" Sadie gushed all at once.

The person on the other end was quiet.

"Ally, I can't hear you, what's up?" Ally was trying to get words out between sobs. "Ally what's happened?"

"Gage...he…"

"What Ally? What did he do?"

"I didn't think he would…I never…" Ally choked out.

"Do what, Ally?" Sadie questioned.

"I upset him, Sadie."

"Where are you? I'm coming over."

"I'm scared Sadie...I'm so scared," she whispered.

159

"Where are you, Ally? Are you at home?"

"Yes."

Sadie hung up the phone, grabbed her bag and keys and raced to the elevators. She didn't notice the text from Levi asking to see her tonight. She had never heard Ally sound this upset before and they had been through a lot together over these last fifteen years. If Gage had hurt her, she'd kill him. She wasn't just her best friend; she was her soul sister, and they had a bond that no man could ever come between.

Chapter 21

Ally

Sadie pulled into Ally's driveway in an area of Toronto referred to as Leslieville twenty minutes later. Rushing to her friend's door, she didn't know what she was going into. She did not like what she heard on the phone and she was stricken with panic and adrenaline.

Ally hid behind the door as she opened it. Sadie entercd, pulling Ally into a hug as they both cried into each other's shoulders. It was dark in the front hall but it wasn't hard to see what was wrong. Gage had hurt her and he had hurt her bad. What Sadie assumed, he not only broke her heart and crushed her spirit, he had left physical bruises to show for it.

"I'm here now. Shhh," she said trying to comfort her best friend. They walked into the kitchen arm in arm where Sadie made some tea. Ally sat down at the kitchen table, her red curls in her hands, tears staining her face. Purple, blue, and green marred her usually flawless skin. Her clear, green eyes were bloodshot.

She went on to tell Sadie everything. Looking back she knew she should have seen it coming, even as early as the first few dates he was controlling everything they did. At first she just thought it was endearing, ordering her drinks and meals, deciding where they would go on dates. By the time they had gone up to his cottage for the long weekend, he was not only controlling what they did, but he started to manipulate her emotionally. Everything she said was wrong, inaccurate, or stupid. He would say hurtful things to make her cry and then apologize profusely, telling her he loved her so much, he didn't know what he was thinking, he was scared of how much he cares for her, that he just wasn't himself around her sometimes. How he will never do it again.

It was exactly how Ally had heard abusive relationships could be. It was stereotypical, and she

READ BETWEEN THE LINES

couldn't believe she stayed as long as she did. It had only been eight months, but long enough. Each time he got aggressive it got worse. First was the emotional manipulation and jealousy, then there was grabbing an arm here or there, and finally what happened this morning.

"Where is he?" Sadie spit out. She was shaking now.

"I have no idea. I acted like I was forgiving him, and then I bolted when he used the washroom. I called you on my way home. He could come here, what if he comes here?" Ally started to panic. She continued crying, "What if he shows up here Sadie?"

"It's okay, it's going to be okay," Sadie said rubbing her back. "Does he know where your mom lives or me?"

"Yes, he knows both of you live in that building."

"Okay, well good thing is Jones won't let him in the building as soon as I give him word. Sam left for L.A. right?"

"She texted from L.A. this morning and honestly, I'm too scared to stay there alone."

163

JILL BREUGEM

"No, I'm staying with you. I'm going to call Levi, we can stay with him. Can I tell him what happened?"

Ally looked at her hands. "You don't think he'll mind? It's embarrassing Sadie."

"You have nothing to be embarrassed of. We should take you to the doctor Ally, get you checked out."

"No, no, I'm fine." Sadie wasn't going to argue with her right now, but knew that they needed to speak to someone. "We should go to the police Ally."

"I really don't want to do that right now. I don't want to go to the police, or the doctor. I just want to put it behind me and forget it," Ally started to cry again. Sadie wrapped her arms around her shoulders. She would address it again later when they were at Levi's, going to the doctor and the police. Ally was too fragile to discuss it now.

"We can talk about that later. Can you quickly go pack a bag? I want to get out of here in case he does come."

Ally agreed and went upstairs to her room to put some things together. Meanwhile Sadie called Levi. He didn't even hesitate and told her he would meet them at Sadie's condo in an hour.

164

READ BETWEEN THE LINES

When they got to Sadie's condo, Ally went to see her mom, while Sadie packed a bag as well. They figured staying at Levi's for a couple days would be best in case Gage had his eye on her mother's condo building. Sadie walked around her bedroom in a daze, unable to believe what had happened. It all felt like a bad dream.

She knew she would need to talk to Ally about charging Gage at some point. She couldn't let him get away with this. As uncomfortable and scary as it was for her, they had to make sure this didn't happen again. She had to make sure that was the last time Ally saw his face or heard his voice.

She threw a toothbrush and a change of clothes in a bag and headed to Catriona's apartment to pick up Ally. Catriona cried as she opened the door and saw her only daughter Ally with bruises on her face. She shrieked and cried and Sadie had to assure her it would not happen again. They would make sure Ally was taken care of. Although not wanting her daughter out of her sight, she agreed that Levi's home was probably the best place until Ally went to the police.

When they arrived at Levi's home, he pulled the car into the garage for extra precaution and they went through the side door that was hidden by a brick wall from the road. They didn't want to risk that Gage could have followed and watched them.

Levi helped get the bags and then gave them their space to talk. He didn't want to make Ally feel uncomfortable or feel that she had to share the details with him. He couldn't understand how a guy could hurt a woman like this. He grew up with parents who barely raised their voice, let alone be abusive to each other.

He had never met Gage. How he would love to meet him now and turn him into the punching bag he had used Ally for. Using violence because of violence was not his style, but the look on Ally's face was enough to get his blood boiling. He was tempted to go look for him but he knew he was best right where he was, just in case there was any way that guy showed up here. Or worse that he end up in jail for what he would do if he did run into Gage.

READ BETWEEN THE LINES

Chapter 22

Late Night Chat

Not wanting to wake up Ally, Sadie tiptoed across the room and closed the door softly behind her. Levi's room was dark and there was a dim light coming from the living room at the bottom of the stairs. She made her way down, grabbed a white chenille throw off of the chair as she entered the room, and curled up on the opposite side of the navy couch. Not looking at her, Levi leaned forward to pick his drink up from the walnut coffee table. The slight ping of the ice clinking in the heavy crystal glass was the only sound in the room. He pushed the silver coaster away from him in a slow motion, let out a big sigh and turned towards Sadie.

"Can't sleep?" he asked and then said, "Me neither."

"No. I just can't believe it. I feel sick for her."

"I know. I just don't understand why someone would want to hurt her. If Oliver finds out about this, he may get arrested."

"Don't tell him, Levi, that would devastate her. "Not our story to tell." Levi put his hand up, knowing it was not the right thing to say.

"No, no, I shouldn't have said that, of course not."

"Okay. Thank you."

"It was a stupid thing to say. I'm sorry."

"It's okay, I realize you were saying it hypothetically. Heck, I want to kill him."

"How's she doing?"

"As good as expected I guess. She tired herself out today, fell asleep fast."

"Looking back, do you think there were signs?"

"Oh definitely."

"Really?"

READ BETWEEN THE LINES

"Yes, I remember feeling uneasy. It all felt so intense."

"How so?"

"Well, Ally said she can see it now too, starting as early as one of their first dates. But somehow, she fell for him anyway, and he would do some really great things. There was good times. It wasn't all bad."

"Do you want a drink? Cup of tea?" Levi offered as he got up and headed into the kitchen.

"I would love a tea." She got up and looked at the pictures of family and friends on the fireplace mantle. She was surprised that Barbara had allowed the picture of the two of them to stay. It was a great picture of them on the sailboat up at the cottage. They were making silly faces and both had red Canada themed bucket hats on their heads. She remembered that day and many others very fondly. There were lots of great memories from the cottage. Except of course the most recent one that she would love to forget. She wondered if he would bring it up again.

Levi interrupted her thoughts while he handed her a mug of tea.

"I just boiled the kettle before you came down. Was going to have a tea, opted for this instead." He shrugged and smiled holding up a tumbler of amber liquid.

"That was a good day," he said, nodding towards the picture of the two of them on the sailboat. "I love that picture."

"Me too," Sadie agreed looking at him softly. "Scotch?" She motioned to his drink.

"Yes, needed something stronger than tea."

"I can understand needing something stronger right now."

"If you only knew…" he muttered under his breath and sat back down. He put his arm on the back of the couch, watching her. He was thinking of the book, what he had read. Did she feel the same or was that just fiction? She still had a boyfriend. He had planned to talk to her about what he read tonight. But he knew it wasn't the right time considering the circumstances with Ally.

"Pardon?" she asked and sat back at the other end of the couch.

"No, no, nothing. What's the plan after the police station? Not that there's any rush to leave here. I quite like the company," he smiled.

"Haven't thought that far yet. I think we'll head to my place or her mom's. I think she can feel

READ BETWEEN THE LINES

confident that he can't hurt her there. Jones will be all over security."

"Well as I said there's no rush."

"Thanks again, Levi. We really appreciate this."

"Sadie, I would do anything for you," he paused looking at her, "and Ally." She knew it, too.

"How does Barbara feel about us being here?"

"Don't know, doesn't matter. Not her business." Wow, she thought, that was harsh.

"Oh? Want to talk about that?"

"Nothing to talk about," he said and went back into the kitchen. He returned a second later and topped up his drink.

"We broke up."

"You did?" Sadie sat up. She was happy and she was stunned. How, when did this happen?

"Couple months back," he answered reading her mind and fell back into the couch. He turned his body, sat under one leg, and looked towards her, waiting to see her reaction.

"Whoa." She knew she still looked stunned, but she really didn't know what to say. "You never said anything…"

171

"There was lots going on at the time," he assured her.

"Did you break up before that night at Plum?" She didn't know if she wanted to know the answer. She had left that night and went right into the arms of Mick, and Levi had had to deal with his dad's illness by himself.

"Yes, we did."

"Ugh," Sadie said, pulling the throw blanket up over her head. He had been alone.

"Sadie?" he said pulling the blanket down to look at her face.

Shaking her head side to side she moaned, "I'm sorry."

"For what?"

"You had to go through everything alone."

"You didn't know."

"But I could've..." she trailed off.

"Could've what?"

She nudged him across the couch with her toe affectionately poking his side.

"Ouch," he said grabbing her foot, placing it under his arm and tickling it. "This, is this what you could've done?!" he teased.

READ BETWEEN THE LINES

"No, Levi! No!!" She squealed through her teeth while trying not to wake Ally. He let go, laughing to himself. "I could've supported you."

"It wasn't your fault that you didn't know about Barbara or my dad. How were you to know? And you have been amazing bringing those meals for my mom and me."

"Why didn't you say something?"

"It wasn't on purpose, just happened to work out that way. Besides, you were enjoying your new relationship. I didn't want to be a downer."

"Levi," she said, saying his name softly to dismiss that thought. He was more important than any relationship she had been in.

"You know what I mean."

"I guess so." She thought about telling him that she'd also broken up with Mick, but hesitated.

"Well, that scotch is putting me to sleep," he said patting her leg. "I'm going to hit the hay." He thought he better call it a night. She was so beautiful lying on his couch, and with the scotch in him he might forget she had a boyfriend.

"Yes, I'll head up too."

173

He turned off the lights and followed her up the stairs, stopping in front of his room. She turned to look at him, her hand on the doorknob.

"Sadie," he said.

"Yes, Levi," her breath caught in her throat and her heartbeat quickened.

He hesitated and then said, "Goodnight, sleep well."

"Goodnight, Levi."

Sadie went and slipped back into bed. She laid on her back looking up at the ceiling. There was a sliver of light coming in from behind the blind. She was confused by Levi's behaviour. He seemed to feel the same. The comment about the picture. The way he looked at her on the couch. The way he looked at her when he said her name before she came back to bed. You could cut the sexual tension with a knife. If he asked her to go with him, she would've. But then he simply said goodnight.

She rolled over in bed, and put her arm around her sleeping best friend. He won't hurt you again Ally, she promised. Her thoughts were going all over the place as she tried to fall asleep. From Ally and Gage, to her writing, to Levi not being with Barbara, to Mick, to no Mick. Levi and Sadie were

READ BETWEEN THE LINES

both single. This had to be a first. In all these years it had to be a first.

It was 3:00 in the morning. She needed to go to sleep before she woke Ally from the tossing and turning beside her. Gingerly getting out of bed, she sat on the floor in lotus pose, her back straight, palms facing up on her knees, closing her eyes to prepare for meditation. The only way she was falling asleep tonight was by clearing her cluttered mind.

Chapter 23

Hope

"You probably think I'm a loser," Ally said to Levi over coffee the next morning. Levi shook his head no, setting his cup down in front of him. He gently put his hand over hers.

"Don't be ridiculous. That guy is a coward. You didn't ask for any of this," he paused then added, "None of this is your fault, no matter what conversations or arguments you had. You know that, right?"

Tears began to stream down Ally's usually cheerful face. She knew it to be true but couldn't help feeling remorseful, sitting in her pajamas in his kitchen, looking and feeling like an absolute wreck. This wasn't who she was. Ally was confident, outspoken, and the life of the party. How did she let that jackass reduce her to this messy puddle she was right now?

"Thanks for letting me stay, Levi."

"Anytime, Ally. Did you sleep well?"

"Yes, thanks I did."

"Good, you are welcome to stay as long as you want."

"Thanks. Won't be long. I'll go back home or to my mom's. Lots to think about."

"For sure. There's really no rush okay?" Waiting for her to nod, he then asked, "Is Sadie up yet?"

"Yes, here I am," Sadie said as she appeared from the hallway.

Levi greeted her with a big smile. "Good morning." Ally watched the exchange between the two of them. It was warm, welcoming and oozed with love. She was thrilled for her best friend, she knew these two couldn't stay away from each other forever. It was only a matter of time and when they finally got together, the stars would finally align. It was going to be magic for them both. One thing

READ BETWEEN THE LINES

about waiting all this time, they had built a solid friendship of respect and trust. Their love was already strong.

"Good morning you two."

Sadie gave Levi a hug and then went over to her best friend to give her one as well. The scent of her shampoo lingered around him after she pulled away. Knowing she had just been in his shower made him start to drift off down a path that would surely cause him embarrassment. He snapped to attention and went to get a glass of water.

"I'm sorry to say there aren't a lot of groceries in the fridge right now. You might find a frost bitten bagel in the freezer to fight over. I will run over to the coffee shop for us. Let me know your orders."

"No, no, I'm not hungry," they said in unison, and then embraced again in a side hug. These two were one in the same, and it didn't surprise him that they had the same answer and said it at the same time. They did that regularly. It was eerie.

"You guys have to eat. Text me a list. I'll pick up some groceries after my meetings today too."

"You're a sweetheart, Levi," Ally gushed. "But my mom messaged and said she wants to do something. She is picking up some things and bringing them by later this afternoon... she will probably bring enough food to last you the year."

"Thanks Catriona," Levi said.

"We're going to take Ally over to the police station to make a statement and see about a restraining order."

"That's a good call. I know it won't be easy for you, Ally, but it's something you need to do," he said, looking at her empathetically and then looking away. He knew how hard this was for her.

"I know it is." Ally got up and headed to her room, leaving Sadie and Levi alone to talk about how pathetic she was, she thought. She knew they wouldn't do it with the intent of hurting her any more than she was, but she couldn't help but feel some anxiety as she exited the kitchen. They wouldn't talk about her in a negative light; Gage was the bad guy and everyone knew it. But it still made Ally look like a lost soul, a helpless child, someone who had been abused. This wasn't Ally. She decided to lift her chin up, straighten her shoulders, and take control. She headed for the shower to get ready for the police station. She was taking her power back.

Chapter 24

Roomies

It was late Saturday afternoon. Ally puttered around the kitchen, making herself at home and placed the salad on the table. It had been a good few weeks here and this was going to be her last weekend. They had fallen into a rhythm and were both very easy going roommates. Levi was gone most days with clients while Ally was writing for papers and filling orders for her essential oil business. Sadie had only stayed a couple nights at the beginning and then went up to the cottage to focus on her writing.

"I was thinking later today we could grab some movies, see if Sadie wants to join us," Levi announced as he walked back into the kitchen from the patio.

"That sounds great." Maybe he would ask Oliver now that he was back in town. She wasn't ready for dating anytime soon, but he was sure nice to look at. Ally remembered the first time she met Oliver. He had been so charming and handsome. He reminded her of a young Marlon Brando, with that smoldering stare, full mouth, and tousled brown hair.

"She was coming back from the cottage today. Unless, she has plans with Mick?"

"Why would she have plans with Mick? They broke up ages ago," Ally answered confused, as she got the cutlery and plates and set the table. Didn't it happen the night Sadie went to see Levi about his dad? Why wouldn't she have told him? Mind you she had no idea until recently he had broke up with Barbara. Wow these two were annoying, she thought in a loving way. They reminded her of Ross and Rachel, always just missing each other, confusing each other, but never able to stay away from each other.

Levi's head snapped towards her. "What?"

READ BETWEEN THE LINES

"What?" Levi was staring at her. She answered his question with a question and sat down in her chair.

"She broke up with Hunky Mick?" He nearly squealed and sat down, got back up and got himself a beer.

"Beer?"

"Sparkling water, please."

"I'm assuming she broke up with him. He was pretty taken with her from what I remember," he said rattling on while handing Ally her drink and sitting back down. Ally smirked to herself, remembering how she typed Hunky Mick in Sadie's phone.

"Yes, so much has been going on, I can't remember the details...but apparently he was getting jealous and clingy." Ally was back to her straightforward self and Levi appreciated it.

"Jealous of what?" he said, hoping it was of him. Maybe Mick had read the book too! What a great book it was, at least what he read. Sadie never had an issue making the reader feel the emotions of what was going on, feel immersed in the story. She had a lot of talent, that's why she sold hit after hit. Fans were ready for more.

183

"I dunno." She shrugged. Except she did. She knew Sadie's relationship with Levi was a point of contention for Mick. It had been for most of Sadie's boyfriends, and she imagined it always would be. But she wasn't about to have that conversation with him, that was Sadie's thing. Even with him looking hopefully at her. It took everything in her to not crumble under his gaze and tell him everything. Sadie was more important to her than anyone in the world, aside from her mom. She would be strong for her. She started to laugh at herself and when she looked up his expression changed from hopeful to concerned.

"Sorry, I just thought of something funny." She took the bowl of salad and piled it high on her plate, and then exchanged it for the plate of chicken.

"So they broke up. Huh. She just never mentioned it." He stuffed a forkful in his mouth, staring straight ahead. He started to smile. He was feeling the way he did when he read the book in her apartment. Unlike Sadie, he wasn't going to give another thought to the fact that she hadn't told him. There had been so much going on. Between visits to his mom and dad, working with clients, and his new houseguest, she may even had told him and he couldn't remember. No. No, he would have remembered that.

READ BETWEEN THE LINES

"Yep." She could barely keep a straight face. She wanted to run out of the room and call Sadie. He felt the same! He felt the same! She always knew he felt the same. He was sitting there smiling at nothing, off in his own little world and it looked like he was having a conversation in his head. He was nodding and tilting his head to the side, just beaming.

"Pretty sure she can do movies," Ally winked at him. He grinned in return.

Just then they both got a text from Sadie.

JILL BREUGEM

Chapter 25

Celebrate

Sadie hit save and closed the lid of her laptop. She was done and she couldn't believe it. She had finished not one, but two books in just a few months. It was crazy. She couldn't write for almost a year and now she had finished two books in mere months? Her editor would probably think they were crap, but she was done. She would worry about it after the first round of editing.

She wanted to celebrate. Picking up her phone she texted a group chat to Levi, Ally, Samantha, Oliver, Piper, and few more to tell them it was party time! Tonight, her place, 8:00, just bring themselves. Her phone was chiming with all of the replies. It looked like everyone was able to make it!

She was so excited. She texted her housekeeper to see if she was free to work this afternoon and run errands. She replied yes instantly. She could always count on Jenny. She texted her a list of sundries, appetizers, groceries for breakfast, and lastly party drinks. This was going to be a good party! Everyone needed a good party these days because there had been so much darkness lately.

What was she going to wear? She felt it had to be something special, knowing that Levi was now single and she wanted to see if it could go somewhere. She did, didn't she? Oh god, her nerves were in her stomach, she felt ill. She flew to the bathroom sink and splashed water on her face. It didn't have to happen tonight. She could enjoy the night with friends. No pressure. Right?!

She circled around her closet until she found a white strapless maxi dress. She was giddy again, she was nervous again, she was freaking out again. She decided to have a long hot bath, glass of wine, and try to calm herself down. She set the condo music to Joni Mitchell's 'Blue' album.

Her phone was still going off with messages but they would have to wait. Her cell wasn't within reach and she was enjoying the bubble bath too much to get out. Her shoulders needed the soak after long days of writing. The feeling of accomplishment was overwhelming and exhausting. Taking a gulp of wine, she sunk into the tub, held her breath and slipped in below the bubbles. Oh man, oh man, tonight could be the night, she thought to herself. She may tell Levi how she was feeling. When she came back up she took another gulp of wine. Pace yourself, Sadie, she mused. You want to be coherent for your own party.

Sadie's book finishing parties were known to be a great time among her circle. Her launch parties were much quieter affairs. There was a local small indie bookstore that Sadie adored. She preferred to have her launch party and first signing there, even though she had reached blockbuster status with her books and big box stores always extended offers.

There was a knock at the door. It must be Jenny. Shoot! She had spent longer than she thought in the tub. Getting out she grabbed a super large towel, wrapped it around herself and put on her housecoat. "Coming Jenny," she called. Extending the door for Jenny to come in, she continued, "I'll just be a few minutes. Let me throw some clothes on."

Sure, I have some groceries to put away. Jones is bringing up the alcohol in ten minutes, "Jenny said.

"Thanks, I'll be right back."

Sadie decided to throw on any old thing for now, as she had lots to do before the party. Checking her messages she had an interesting one from Ally.

"Levi didn't know you broke up with Mick. What is up with you guys, do you ever talk?"

"Been a lot going on, it just was never a good time to say."

"Well it looks like he is happy about it!" Ally answered.

"Really? Can I call you?!" Sadie was freaking out again. She needed to speak to her best friend and understand what went on. What was the conversation, how did it go, how did it come up?

"No, I'm sitting at the table with him, having lunch!" Ally replied.

"Okay, I have to get ready for the party. Let's sneak away at some point, I want to know every detail!"

"You got it :) "

READ BETWEEN THE LINES

Sadie set her phone down and finished getting dressed. Ally sat her phone face down, turned to Levi and said, "I think tonight's going to be a lot of fun."

Chapter 26

Party

Ally and Levi were the first to arrive with their arms full of surprises. Ally was holding 'You did it!' and 'Congratulations' balloons, and a box of cupcakes from Sadie's favourite bakery. Levi had a bouquet of Sadie's favourite roses. They were called Mimi Eden Roses and there was only a handful of florists in the city that would carry them. She absolutely loved them because they reminded her of an old English garden. She stood in the middle and hugged Ally and Levi at the same time in a group hug, then kissed them both on the cheeks. She noticed how amazing Levi smelled.

JILL BREUGEM

"Haha, thank you! Yummy! Ally, you know how much I love these!" and then turning to Levi, "Thank you! You always spoil me with flowers, but never these, these are my absolute favourite flower. Beautiful, Levi."

"I'm thrilled you're done the book. When can I have a peek at it?" he said smiling.

"Oh, within the next few days, but not tonight. No work tonight." She danced away from them to put the flowers in a vase and the cupcakes on a platter. The cupcakes from Ally she understood, but Levi got her her favourite flowers? "What can I get you two to drink?"

Just as she asked there was a knock at the door with more guests arriving. She had given Jones a guest list so he could send them up as they arrived and not have to check in. "Go ahead and help yourself, I'll get the door," she said while dancing silly past them, making them both laugh.

"Oliver! You're back! I texted you just in case, so glad you could make it!" She hugged him and immediately looked back to see Ally smiling from ear to ear. Sadie led him in over to Ally and Levi.

"Hey brother, how are you?" The two best friends hugged. Oliver then turned to Ally and smiled. He took her hand in a sweet handshake, covering her hand with his free one, and then pulling her into a hug"

"It's great to see you again Ally."

"You too, Oliver, you're keeping well." She winked at him. Ally the confident flirt was back, and Sadie was thrilled. She knew Ally was not in a place to start dating yet, but there was no reason she couldn't have a good time. Oliver was the man to deliver. The sparks that were flying between the two of them as they went on to chat effortlessly was enchanting. Sadie looked past them to Levi. He was looking right at her, and she felt her face heat up, her stomach fill with butterflies. It was funny how he could turn her into a pile of goo, just with a look. The knock at the door saved her the embarrassment of her red face just in time, although she was sure he caught it.

"Sam!" She hugged her friend and pulled her into the apartment, greeting Sam's date at the same time.

"Sadie this is Adam, Adam this is one of my bestest, Sadie."

"Great to meet you, Adam," Sadie said, extending her hand. There went her face again, turning several shades as she realized she was meeting THE Adam Lane, a famous Hollywood actor. Oh Sam, she could have warned me, she laughed to herself.

"Great to meet you, Sadie. I've heard so much about you."

"Please come on in, thanks so much for coming." Sadie led them over to Levi, Oliver, and Ally, and watched their mouths slightly drop as they realized who they were in the presence of. She giggled to herself, happy she wasn't the only star struck one there.

"Can I get you a drink, Adam?" Sadie asked.

"Sure, beer would be great. This is a great place, look at that view," Adam said, as he walked towards the windows that faced downtown. It was after 9:00 and the skyline was lit up. It was really an exceptional sight.

"It was one of the reasons I chose this space. I love this city."

"It's my first time here. Sam is going to take me on some touristy adventure tomorrow."

"Well, I know that Toronto is a little easier to get around with some anonymity."

"I asked her if we need to have some wigs and disguises, just in case - but she says it's not necessary here."

READ BETWEEN THE LINES

"Well, if you wear any kind of disguise please send me a picture of that," Sadie joked as she walked Adam back over to the group.

"I'll grab your beer. Sam, do you want to do introductions?" She interrupted her friend who was making the rounds hugging everyone.

"Of course!" Grabbing Adam by the arm, she pulled him in close and introduced him to everyone.

More and more guests arrived and soon it was a full house of good friends having a great time. They were there to help celebrate. Sadie had thrown herself these parties after each book. Her friends came to expect them and look forward to them.

"Hey girl!" Piper shrieked as she took Sadie in a big hug. Piper smelled of jasmine and citrus, likely a concoction made by Ally.

"You smell divine, Piper!"

"You as well...Ally make it?"

"Of course!"

"Can't wait to read your book Sadie, so excited you're done. Are you coming by next week?"

"Yes, I think Levi has something set up."

"Fantastic! So how is Levi anyway?"

"He's doing pretty well, why?"

"Don't play coy with me Miss Sadie…I see the sparks fly between you two, and I happen to know you're both single right now."

"You heard about Mick?" Sadie looked down, feeling terrible. Mick was Piper's friend she had met at Piper's barbeque.

"Oh don't give it another thought. There's someone for everyone and I know who yours is, and it's not Mick. And Mick will be just fine."

Sadie looked up and past her friend, right into the eyes of Levi. He looked as if he had been waiting for her. She smiled first with her eyes, then it drew upon the corners of her mouth in slow motion as if they were having a staring contest and she had just lost. He smiled back. They stayed locked in the gaze for several moments. She felt the heat in her cheeks and churn in her belly from the intimate moment they just shared. Piper followed the look on Sadie's face right to the man in question. "Wow," Piper leaned forward and whispered in Sadie's ear. "Do you want us all to leave?"

Sadie broke eye contact, and swatted Piper away laughing. "Stop it."

"Whatever, he's coming this way." Sadie's head whipped around to see that he was in fact walking straight for her.

READ BETWEEN THE LINES

"Hey, Piper, how are you?" Levi asked as he approached them, gently sliding his hand into Sadie's hand as he came closer.

"I'm spectacular, Levi, you?" she said with a wink.

"Fantastic. I think we have a really good book to share with you next week." He beamed. Sadie looked at him, confused. He barely knew what the book was about, how could he comment on it to Piper? She was planning on sharing the story of the photographer with him before they saw Piper.

"Can't wait!" Piper exclaimed. She air kissed them both and made her way over to her boyfriend, slinking her arms around his body, leaning into his chest for a hug. Sadie wanted that, she wanted that so bad.

"Good party, Sadie." He paused, "Listen, I need to talk to you about something when you get a chance."

"Oh, is everything okay?" she asked.

"Yes, everything is fine, maybe after everyone leaves?"

"Keeping me in suspense until then?" She raised one eyebrow.

199

Chuckling, he faced her and ran his hands up her arms. "I don't want to keep you from your party, it can wait." He squeezed her arms and they headed back over to Oliver and Ally, who hadn't moved an inch since arriving.

Chapter 27

The Kiss

Sadie closed the door after Ally and Oliver, the last guests to leave, except Levi. She had no doubt Oliver would make sure that Ally got home safely on the next floor to her mom Catriona's. Sadie couldn't wait to talk to Ally tomorrow about Oliver and the details she was supposed to share about Levi. She couldn't pry her away from Oliver all night.

Levi was busy in her kitchen, putting dishes into the dishwasher and the empty bottles into a recycle bin. She stopped at the island and watched him. He was looking incredibly sexy cleaning up after the party for her. He caught her looking so she started to busy herself with dishes on the table.

"You don't have to do this Levi, I can take care of it in the morning."

"It's no problem at all. Hey do you want a tea, I just started the kettle." He knew her so well.

"I would love one." She picked platters up off of the dining table and brought to the sink to rinse off. "Hey, didn't you say you have something to talk to me about?"

He looked up from the coffee table with empty bottles in his hand.

"Yes, I do," he said with some hesitation in his voice.

"Okay, do you want to talk now?" She could sense the pause. She turned around to face him.

Coming around and standing behind her at the sink, he leaned back against the island. His broad shoulders and strong arms were bracing his body with his large hands. His navy V-neck was showing just enough of his tanned, smooth chest to make Sadie lose her focus. His worn jeans were sitting on his hips, his legs crossed at the ankles. His head was cocked to the side, showing off his smooth neck. He was gorgeous.

READ BETWEEN THE LINES

'Into the Mystic' started playing over the speakers. Taking one of her hands in his, he tugged her towards him and pulled her in close. "Dance with me," he whispered in her ear. Sadie didn't miss a beat, and wrapped her arms around his neck, as his hands came to rest on her hips. Her heart was beating so loud, she could hear it pounding in her ears. They starting moving around her kitchen and then into the living room, in a slow rhythmic dance. It was incredibly romantic, two best friends finally finding each other after all this time. Most of the lights in the condo were off except for a dim light over the stove. As the song ended they came to a stop in front of the large windows facing the city's skyline.

The dancing stopped, but neither one let go. They felt so good together. Sadie rested her head against his chest, Levi pulled her tighter into a hug. Her breathing calmed. Sighing, he stepped back enough to look in her eyes, to her mouth, and back into her eyes.

Then it happened. Moving his hands up her body, he cupped her face, while her hands fell and came to rest on his chest. The kiss was everything she imagined and more. Soft but firm, his kiss took her to a place she had only ever hoped to go. As her insides curled a small moan escaped her. He kissed her harder. He moved his hands to the back of her neck, up into her hair. Wow. She could hardly breathe. Then he pulled away.

"Sadie, I have a confession to make." Suddenly he was afraid of how she was going to react. What if she was angry that he had read it? He hadn't even thought about it until this moment. Now he was worried about how she would respond. That kiss was so amazing, he knew that it was going to lead to much more. But it was Sadie, he felt he had to say something.

"A confession?" She felt a pang, a nauseas pang. What could it be? Barbara? Someone else?

He took her hands in his. His strong warm hands, wrapped around her wrists, down the backs of her soft hands and resting with their palms together and fingers linked. Looking down at them he took a deep breath and started. What was he about to say, she wondered. The feeling of his lips was still on hers, her body still reacting to him.

"I…" He paused. "I read the book."

"What?" What was he saying, which book? She was beginning to feel anxious.

"I read THE book." He looked in her eyes. He looked down at her hands. He looked back up in her eyes. Still holding her hands.

READ BETWEEN THE LINES

He explained further, "I read the book about us."

Sadie pulled back, folded her arms close to her body and walked away. Trying to stay calm, her mind began racing. When? How? What?

He followed her. Trying to give her the space she needed to digest the information before continuing with how he had read it. Knowing Sadie, and knowing how she felt when he read her work before she was ready to share it, he was now 100% terrified of how she was going to react. Her body language told him he was in trouble. What had he done?

"What do you mean, the book about us?" she spat out. She was so confused, how could he have read it. It was so personal. She didn't know if it was ever going to see the light of day.

"I read a book that I know is about the two of us. There were specific memories you wrote about, I…"

Cutting him off she said sternly, "HOW exactly did you come across this book?"

"Sadie, please don't be mad, I loved it...I…"

"HOW exactly did you come across this book, Levi?"

"About a month ago, when I brought dinner over for you. You had gone out to an appointment." Her eyebrows were raising and her smile was long gone. "You left your laptop open." He was looking at the floor again.

"That was a month ago Levi." she hissed. Feeling exposed and disappointed, she no longer felt the warmth of moments ago, nor felt like his company or hearing anymore. A defense mechanism was kicking in; Sadie was shutting down. "You should go."

"Sadie, let me explain what happened," he pleaded, walking towards her.

"No thanks. I'm tired. You can let yourself out."

Leaving him standing in her living room, she went to her bedroom and slammed the door. Perhaps dramatic she thought, but she had a message she wanted to send him. He knew her limits when it came to her books. He knew that she was a private person and he had violated it when he looked at her laptop. Lastly he had a month, and many opportunities to tell her that he read it. She felt like a fool. A big, bitchy fool.

She went to her closet and changed into yoga capris and a tank top and crawled onto her bed.

READ BETWEEN THE LINES

She knew she should go and wash her face, but she didn't have the will or the want to. She heard the front door close and the lock click into place. She closed her eyes, a single tear sliding down her cheek as she faded off to sleep.

Chapter 28

Forgiveness

"Are you sure you want to do this, Ally?" Sadie asked.

"Yes, I'll feel better. My mom will feel better. It doesn't have to be long term." Ally shuffled around her kitchen, packing boxes.

"You don't have to worry about him anymore, you know that right?"

"I know. But, it's a new chapter. I want to open a shop and this will free up some funds for that."

It had been months since the incident with Gage and Ally had taken refuge at Levi's. Sadie had only stayed the first night. She needed to focus on writing and knew Ally didn't need her hovering over her every move. While Ally had stayed there, she had come up with some plans. First was selling her first home and moving back in with her mom for a while. Security was good at the building, and they felt they didn't have to worry about Gage. He not only took the restraining order well, he also headed back out west to live with his family. Admitting it was a bad mistake, fuelled by alcohol, he had committed to getting help. Regardless of whether or not they could trust the Gage would stay away, Ally was not one to live her life in fear.

The second part of her plans would be setting up a shop to sell her essential oils. It was time to do what she really enjoyed and she knew from her current customers that she could really try to make a go of it. She thought about locations around the city, and settled on an area in a trendy area called the Beach. Rent would be high, but the clientele would be perfect for her concoctions.

"When are you going to forgive him, Sadie?"

"Who?" Sadie asked, nonchalantly.

"Sadie…" She knew what Ally was talking about. It had been a couple months since Sadie had had her party, since Levi kissed her and had thrown her emotions into a spin. It was the happiest she had been in a long time, it was finally happening for them, dancing around her apartment and holding each other close. The kiss had been amazing. In seconds it had all turned upside down. He confessed to reading her book about them on her laptop when she wasn't home. She was angry that he had read it at all, that he hadn't closed her laptop knowing how she would feel, and she felt betrayed because he had had plenty of time to tell her. She felt vulnerable to the situation, thinking of how he must have looked at her in the days following, because if he had felt the same why hadn't he said something right away?

Levi had tried to reach out, texting and leaving voice messages daily at the beginning. She knew he wanted to talk and sort things out, but she wasn't quite ready. She went about her business meetings without him, meeting with the editor, final decisions on the cover, seeing Piper, and setting dates for interviews and promotion. She asked him not to attend and to give her space, and he had.

"Sadie, he's really sorry," Ally pleaded.

"What time is the moving van coming tomorrow?"

"Sadie, he loves you, and I know you feel the same. Yes he made poor judgement but," Ally started to explain, "I know that if you listen to him you will understand that there just wasn't a good time to tell you. You two had just started talking again and then Gage happened."

Deep down Sadie knew this. She knew that she should forgive him and talk to him, but she had let days turn into weeks and weeks turn into two months. She had let it go too long and now didn't know what to say. She was letting self-doubt creep in, reminding herself that if he truly had felt the same, he could have found some moment to tell her?

"I know there may not have been a good time, but if you just read a story about you and someone," she said, pausing for effect, "a private and autobiographical novel -- a memoir if you will - - that basically professes their love for you...wouldn't you say something no matter what was going on? Especially if you felt the same?"

"Yes, maybe, I don't know." Ally whispered.

"Well, if he felt the same, I would think he would've. So, if he doesn't feel the same, I need space from him right now, because I can't stand the thought." But had he said he felt the same when he told her that night? She was so angry that night that she couldn't remember.

"Sadie, I know he feels the same. Why don't you just call him? Hear him out?" Ally said.

READ BETWEEN THE LINES

"I don't know..."

"Think about it?" Ally tilted her curly, ginger head to the side, and looked at her with her big green eyes. Sometimes those eyes looked like the emerald isles. She pictured a young Alison running through the fields of the Antrim Coast in Northern Ireland where she was born. After her mom became pregnant with the famous baseball player, she went back home to Northern Ireland to have her baby. She returned to Canada several years later to stay for good. Running back home had proved to not be the sanctuary she needed, and she found this is where they belonged.

Sadie looked at her best friend. She had been through so much, and yet she was already moving on from Gage, having long since forgiven him. Although Ally was not one to put up with anything, she also felt it would only hurt her to stay angry. She made a point of forgiving everyone. Even Gage.

So it felt ridiculous to be holding onto this bitter pill, when Levi's heart was likely in the right place at the time. She may have to swallow disappointment and rejection from Levi. She knew for everyone's sake (including her own) she needed to move on and make peace. Not talking to him was affecting everybody. She also needed an agent with

213

impending book launch. Sadie walked over to her phone, and texted a quick message to Levi. "My launch party is on November 1st at 8:00 at the Cafe. Hope to see you there. S"

Before she could set the phone down he had responded, "Wouldn't miss it." She instantly felt relieved. Thank you for that Levi, she thought.

"There, I just texted him, asked him to come to my launch party. He said yes."

"That's great, Sade!"

"Well, we'll see if it's that great…"

"It will be. I know it."

"Hey, how's Oliver?"

"Oh he's good. We've been seeing a bit of each other."

"Really? Even though you told him you weren't interested in rushing into anything after Gage?" She knew her friend needed to take things slow.

"Yes," pausing to tape up a box and move it to the pile in the front room. "We are having a good time." Sadie could see the smile break across her friend's face as she was thinking about him. "He's a great guy."

READ BETWEEN THE LINES

Sadie was happy for her. She wanted Ally to be involved for the right reasons though and worried it was too soon. Before Gage, Ally didn't have a lot of long term relationships. She wondered if this was just a passing fling to help get over Gage. Maybe that was okay too.

"Yes, always liked Oliver," Sadie confirmed.

"Maybe he'll come to your launch party?"

Picking up her phone again, Sadie texted a quick note to Oliver asking him to come to the launch party in a few days. Ally was like a young schoolgirl, giggling and looking over Sadie's shoulder at the text. Sadie dropped the phone into her pocket and said, "Okay, now that that's out of the way, let's focus! We have lots to do!"

Chapter 29

Launch Party

It was November first and the launch party was tonight at a local coffee house bookstore. Sadie hopped out of bed with the excitement of a child on Christmas morning. She had lots to do to prep for the day. Looking at her phone, she saw she already had a few messages from her friends and family congratulating her on the release of her new book. She was missing a text from one person, and that weighed heavy on her heart. She hadn't heard from Levi since asking him to come to the launch party.

There was a big surprise in store for everyone there tonight, except Piper who had been in on it the whole time. Shooting Piper a message she asked if there was anything she could do to help with the night's festivities. It was going to be a little lower key than other years and that was good by Sadie. After all, she had published several books over the years and had had many launch parties; friends and family didn't need to attend them all. Tonight the plan was for a small gathering of her close friends. In the coming days they would have another event at a larger big box chain bookstore with print media and fans. And then there would the book tour at the end of the month.

"Can't wait for tonight, Sade! One box of books have been delivered for the event." Piper replied.

"Fantastic, see you tonight!" Sadie answered.

The day flew and before she knew it she was heading over to the event with Ally. Sadie was wearing a short red wrap dress, with nude Louboutin heels and diamond stud earrings. Her arms and hands were bare except for the sheer polish on her manicured nails. Her hair was blown out in sexy waves and her makeup was done with natural tones except for a solid line of black liner on her upper eyelid. She felt phenomenal and by the way Ally looked at her when they met in the lobby she knew she had achieved the look she was going for.

Sadie smiled brightly at her gorgeous bestie. Ally was a stunner in body hugging nude lace dress and heels to match. Her beautiful face was framed with auburn curls and just a touch of mascara to darken her thick eyelashes that framed her emerald green eyes. The driver gave them both genuine nods assisting them in the car. They were fortunate that the snow hadn't come yet and they were enjoying warmer than seasonal temps.

They entered the dimly lit shop and noticed how romantic it looked. Candles were lit on antique glass chandeliers and her favourite roses were placed throughout the room. Piper was already there passing out wine glasses and pouring Sadie's favourite red. Taking a quick glance around she noticed that Levi wasn't there yet.

"Sadie! Whoa! HOT!" Piper exclaimed. "You're not giving him a chance tonight!" Knowing exactly who Piper was referring to. Sadie chuckled at her comment. Piper always knew the right thing to say.

Leaving Ally with Piper, Sadie slowly walked to the table with the display of books. They looked beautiful. The sight was just as much a surprise to Sadie as they would be for everyone else. It was the first time she was seeing her work in person. She always felt her books were like her babies, and this time was no different. Except it was very, very different. This book was very personal and it meant more than any that had come before. This book rivalled her first book in importance, and that book changed her life, could this one as well? She picked a book up and ran her hand up the front and the back, the spine, then held it close to her body, inhaling the paper scent. This was love.

"I hate to interrupt your thoughts, but Levi has just arrived. Thought you might want to know," Ally whispered to her friend. Sadie was completely oblivious that the room had filled up around her. People were chatting, drinking wine, and enjoying hors d'oeuvres. All of her closest friends and fellow writers had gathered here for her; she was grateful and humbled.

Turning slowly towards the door, Sadie looked for him in the dim light. Her body, filled with nerves, took comfort upon seeing him. He was in conversation with Piper but he looked distracted. He seemed as nervous as Sadie was feeling, trying to steady the hands he was rubbing on his upper legs. He was as handsome as ever. He was wearing a tailored, fitted, black dress shirt and pants, and his

READ BETWEEN THE LINES

thick, wavy, blonde hair was slicked back for the occasion.

She waited until their eyes met and waved hello. He mouthed the word hi, giving her a broad smile, and without taking his eyes off of her, made his way across the room to where she stood, still cradling a book.

"Hi Sadie, congratulations." He leaned in and kissed her on the cheek, his familiar scent having the same effect as always on her.

"Hi, Levi. Thanks for coming." She fanned her hand around the room, as if there were another reason he would be there.

"You know I wouldn't miss it." He paused and then moved in closer to say in her ear, "Sadie...you are absolutely breathtaking."

"As are you," she answered with a squeak, coming apart from his breathe on her neck. She grabbed the table behind her to steady herself with one hand and with the other, shakily handed Levi a book. This is it.

"I'm just going to say a few words, I'll be back". Somewhat taken aback by the cover of the book, not being the one she had shown him about the photographer, he looked down at the book and back up at Sadie. She was already gone.

221

Piper was ready for her, she gave a quick introduction to the crowd, and handed her a microphone and a fresh glass of wine.

"I would like to thank all of you for being here tonight for the release of my seventh book." Sadie took a sip of her wine as the audience clapped. Setting down the glass on an antique table to her side she swallowed slowly, trying to calm herself before continuing. The top of the table was scarred and bumpy and she didn't know if it was the shaking of her hands or the markings that caused the glass to tip a little before settling in. She took a full deep breath in, and deep breath out, and reminded herself of the quote 'Everything you want is on the other side of fear'. She knew for herself this was true.

What might have been an uncomfortable amount of time to pass for some was not for Sadie. She wanted to get her message across clearly and sincerely.

"This book is very special to me, and for those who know me well, will understand the plot and characters to be very close to my heart. You see, this book took seven years to write. Not intentionally of course, sometimes the words are right in front of you, sometimes they don't make sense, and

READ BETWEEN THE LINES

sometimes you just need to give in to the process and read between the lines."

Sadie made a point of looking around the room, into the eyes of her audience, and landing on Levi.

"Fear has stopped me from exploring these words in the past, from enjoying the story that was developing right before my eyes all these years," she continued.

"I hope it isn't too late to share the story with you." Deliberately looking at Levi, she stood a little taller, and smiled as he moved through the crowd towards her.

"Thanks again for coming everyone, enjoy the drinks and food, and the rest of your evening." The crowd clapped as Levi pulled her into his arms. First he hugged her tight, then he leaned down and gave her a kiss. The crowd roared with approval. Sadie thought she could even hear someone yell "It's about time!"

Chapter 30

The Envelope

With several local interviews and the launch party behind her, Levi and Sadie decided to head up to the cottage for a couple days before Sadie had to start touring. They were sitting on the deck in front of the outdoor fireplace, overlooking the lake on a crisp fall evening. Wrapped in his grandmother's quilts on oversized Muskoka chairs, they enjoyed a bottle of wine while sharing stories from over the years.

"Remember when you and Barbara got into it over the best type of hostess gift to give my mother?" Levi chided and continued, "I was looking back and forth as the two of you argued, wine, flowers, wine, flowers...I thought you were going to hit her!"

Sadie let out a big laugh. "It wasn't quite like that..." Sadie said under her breath. "But we didn't see eye to eye on much. I just couldn't warm up to her."

"What was it about her?" Levi inquired.

"Ugh, everything. She was so snobby, so high maintenance, she took advantage of you. And she hated me!" she exclaimed laughing.

"Yes, that she did." Levi said, laughing along with her. No need to deny it when they both knew it to be true. "She always thought we secretly wanted more than a friendship. She would say I was taking your side all the time."

"Oh really?"

"She was probably right."

"Oh come on now...she was your girlfriend."

"Well, we were, are, close, Sadie. I would be lying if I said I never thought about what it would be like to be more than friends all these years." Levi looked at his wine, swirling it in the glass.

Continuing, he said, "I think I fell in love with you the first time we met, and Oliver knew that was going to happen to me when he set it up." Looking

READ BETWEEN THE LINES

down at his wine and back up at her he said, "He warned me."

Sadie was blushing; of course she had felt the same. They had sat talking for hours that first night, neither making the move to say good night.

Then he added, "Then there was a time shortly after that, we went out with Oliver and Piper and the crew. If I remember correctly, we danced a lot." Sadie shook her head yes, remembering that memory very well. He added, "But were both dating other people."

"Yes. And had started working together, too," she pointed out.

"Mmmhmm," he agreed. "Do you know when it really hit me though?"

"When?" Sadie said, leaning in closer.

"Remember when we were in your bedroom, lying on your floor, actually I think it was in your closet, and we read all of your journals from when you were a kid?"

"Yes, I do. You know that, that's in the book." She winked and smiled at him.

"Yes, I know." Levi took her hand and kissed the back of it, placing it gently on his lap with his hand covering it.

227

"I need to show you something. Come inside."
He tugged gently on her hand, leading her into the cottage, both of them with the blankets still around their shoulders. Levi let go of her hand and went to a small drawer in the kitchen and pulled out an envelope. Sadie went and sat down on the couch, really intrigued by the envelope.

"What is it, Levi?" she asked, pulling the blankets around her. She could faintly smell the campfire smell from the last time they were at the cottage.

He handed an envelope to Sadie, and sat down on the coffee table facing her, running his hands through his thick hair. Bringing his hands in front of him, he let out a big sigh, smiled, and motioned for her to open it.

"What is this?" she asked again, returning his smile.

"Open it," he nodded, leaning forward to be put his elbows on his knees, clasping his large hands in front of him.

Looking questionably at Levi, she ran her fingers along the manila envelope, flipped it over, and opened the flap carefully to pull out some legal documents. Totally confused, Sadie began to read the fine print.

READ BETWEEN THE LINES

"You came with me when I bought it, you've been the constant presence by my side enjoying this place over the years, and if it weren't for you, I wouldn't have it."

Sadie eyes welled up with tears as she realized it was the deed to the cottage, and that he had put her name on it.

"Levi?" Looking at him with her mouth agape, in shock, and tears running down her face, she pushed the blankets off and stood up in front of him. He pulled her onto his lap, wrapped his arms around her and whispered, "Don't cry" into her hair.

Lifting her head from his shoulder she said, "I don't know what to say. This is amazing. I love this place."

"You love it as much as I do. I wouldn't have it if it weren't for you, Sadie."

The lights were off in the cottage but the music was playing. Blue Rodeo's 'Rain Down on Me' started to play. The song had reminded her of Levi for years; she remembered the first time she had heard it at the cottage.

Sadie turned her face towards him, wrapped her arms around his neck, then Levi leaned forward and kissed her. It was urgent and romantic, like he didn't know if he would ever have this opportunity again. Sadie stepped back, Levi let go of her arms and moved his hands to cradle her face. He whispered her name and leaned down to give her a soft, sensual kiss that went right to her knees. Sadie moved her arms up his chest and clenched his shirt in her fists. She couldn't help the moan that escaped her, and Levi clearly didn't mind as he pulled her even closer and backed her up against door. His hands moved from her face down to her shoulders, down her arms, and then to her waist. Sadie had to remind herself to breathe.

Levi pulled away for a moment, meeting her gaze. They both smiled.

"I love you, Sadie."

"I love you, too, Levi."

Made in the USA
Charleston, SC
18 February 2017